Imprisoned Hearts

Book 2 of the Hidden Hearts Series

Macy Lewis

ARCHWAY
PUBLISHING

Archway Publishing books may be ordered through booksellers or by contacting:

Archway Publishing
1663 Liberty Drive
Bloomington, IN 47403
www.archwaypublishing.com
844-669-3957

Cover Image Credit: Madeleine Kmetzsch

ISBN: 978-1-4808-9430-3 (sc)
ISBN: 978-1-4808-9431-0 (e)

Library of Congress Control Number: 2020915109

Print information available on the last page.

Archway Publishing rev. date: 08/28/2020

ACKNOWLEDGEMENTS

I would like to thank the following people for their help with this book.

Jim King, thank you for the numerous telephone conversations, reading the manuscript, offering suggestions, and for always believing in me.

Madeleine Kmetzsch, thank you for the book cover, it is beautiful!

Kelly Mattingly, M.Ed., your expertise on sexual assault and human trafficking was invaluable. Thank you for the numerous telephone conversations and ensuring my writing sounded authentic as you weaved numerous ideas together on the final draft. Thank you for your encouragement, I could not have written this book without you!

Samantha Moeai, M.S.W., your expertise on sexual assault was invaluable. Thank you for the support, the articles and textbook suggestions, for reading my work and helping it sound authentic. Rebecca, thank you for being my liaison to Samantha. You were the link that made her help happen.

Lisa Ford, thank you for answering my numerous questions and explaining the British education system, which made this book more authentic. I am so grateful for your friendship and support!

Claire Hux, Gina Strickland, and Lorin Nicholson, thank you for helping with British terms, phrases, and advice on the legal system which made this book more authentic. I could not write without you!

Trishelle Duncan, thank you for helping me finish the recipe for Buttered Bliss. Thank you for the encouragement, you are such a light in my life!

Kate Larimer, thank you for reading the manuscript, offering suggestions, and for your support!

Traci McDonald, thank you for the support and mentorship as I wrote this book.

Janelle Evans, thank you for doing a final edit on the manuscript, catching everything I missed and adding more depth. You made this book even better than I could have imagined!

Dad, thank you for going through the manuscript with me and accepting Janelle's edits, I could not have done it without you!

Christopher, Lily, Lindsey, Gabby, Don James, Debbie, Spencer, Jarom and Michelle, Megan, Brett, Erica, Lynda, and Annette, thank you for the help and encouragement.

Archway Publishing, thank you for the help publishing this book.

To all my friends and family, thank you for the support. I am so blessed to have you in my life.

Contents

CHAPTER 1

Closing the door, I went to my bed and sat down. The papers I discovered two weeks earlier were finally in my hands, and I vowed never to let them out of my sight. The papers were correspondence from my mother, Beatrice, to a man named Jack Julian. The letters, dated seventeen-and-one-half years ago, mentioned that she thought the child she carried was his, but they would never be together because she found Mr. Right in someone else. The man asked for a paternity test and she obliged. The results? I had no idea. They weren't here.

The smell of alcohol and smoke drifted through the air vent and beneath the door, making my head spin and my stomach turn. It burnt my throat, choking me. I needed fresh air but couldn't find any. The rumpus coming from the floor beneath my bedroom made focusing on the contents of the letters nearly impossible. The music mixed with the shouts of four rowdy couples disturbed my already foggy thoughts. The light from the floor lamp at the foot of my bed cast shadows around the small, empty bedroom. My threadbare blankets offered little relief to the chill creeping through the cracks in the dirty window, though bits of moonlight did make it through the grimy glass.

I rubbed my temples and played with my shoulder-length, curly, black hair, looking over my chemistry and history homework. Placing the books and papers that were strewn on the bed into my backpack, I slid my pack to the floor and pulled my knees into my chest. I rested my aching head on my knees, listening to Beatrice, her freeloading fiancé, Miguel, and their friends drinking and shooting up. The thought of all those illegal drugs down there made me shiver.

I tensed with every tramping footstep that ascended the creaking staircase. A lump formed in my throat and tears in the back of my bloodshot eyes at the fear of being attacked by one of those high and drunk men who came upstairs to use the toilet next door. My skyrocketing adrenaline sent blood pumping through my veins, tightening my stomach into knots and increased my breathing. Cringing underneath the thin blankets, I felt trickling, icey fingers roll down my body.

Even though it's nearly twelve-thirty in the morning, you'll go to Lisi's after Edgington, and you won't have to come back here for a while.

My thoughts drifted to Kahleesi, my best friend who I called Lisi, and her mother Krisany, who I called Krissy. Beatrice's friend in secondary school, Krisany had been more like a mother to me than Beatrice ever was. But she wasn't here now. More footsteps ascended the stairs and I hear Miguel slurring something to Beatrice. Those footsteps seemed to stop outside my door and the doorknob began to turn. My blood turned to frozen slush. Shaking with fear, I slid to the edge of the bed until my knees and arms touched the dirty wall. Hot tears fell from my eyes as I pled with God to keep Miguel away from me.

He doesn't know what he's doing. He's so high, he could kill me if he gets in here. There's no way I'm letting him touch me. I'll fight him and get away.

My nails dig into my folded arms…waiting, clenching my jaw harder at every noise. Thankfully, Miguel used the toilet and went tramping down the stairs. My body shook with silent sobs of relief at his receding footsteps.

No seventeen-year-old girl should have to endure this hell. I can't take it anymore!

Stretching out on the bed, I lay motionless, listening to the mayhem below. I didn't dare fall into a deep sleep, for fear of what the men might do. My stomach rumbled. I hadn't been hungry before the house party, but, now several hours later, my starving body desperately wanted something to eat and drink. But no way would I show my face amongst the party goers.

When I was younger, Beatrice locked me in my bedroom so I couldn't show my face to her friends, even though they all knew about me. Or, at least, she told me they knew about me. Beatrice had told me so many lies, I wasn't sure what to believe anymore. The only adult I trusted was Krisany.

I looked at the hands on my watch. After 1:30 a.m. The last of Beatrice's friends had left and she and Miguel went to their room to make love. Feeling the vomit coming, I got out of bed, hefted my backpack, took the few clothing items from the dust-caked empty wardrobe across the room, and walked down the stairs. I didn't want Beatrice or Miguel to discover the papers, which I had taken.

The noise from Beatrice and Miguel's lovemaking drowned out all sounds of the staircase creaking beneath my feet. At the bottom of the stairs, I was mortified by what I saw. Empty alcohol bottles, drug paraphernalia, food, and dirty dishes littered the house. I couldn't believe the rubbish from one party, but I didn't stick around to clean up. Walking into the kitchen, I opened the refrigerator and retrieved the pizza Beatrice ordered for me so I wouldn't interrupt her lovemaking after the party adjourned.

I made my way down the dimly lit cellar staircase. A place where I always felt safer, but it didn't have a toilet. I had to choose wisely when to come down here.

The air rank with must and mold grew colder, and I started to shiver. I sat on the dirty, black, leather settee in the corner of the barren, concrete room. In the dim yellow light, bugs crawled up and down the moist walls, but I didn't care. I focused on the cold pizza, cramming it into my mouth. My stomach churned due to my nerves from the night, but I kept swallowing down mouthfuls of pizza. It would be the only meal I would have until lunch.

I set the empty pizza box on the cold concrete at my feet and wrapped the clothes around me. My body shook from head to toe from the cold air.

"Alice Brianna Esposito," Miguel's shout two floors above made me freeze. "Where the hell are you?"

I couldn't resist sneaking up the cellar stairs to peer around the corner, to look at the staircase leading to the first floor. Miguel stood at the top, leaning against the wall for support. His burning red face and eyes darted around the dark room, trying to find me in the darkness. The veins popping out of his forehead mixed with the sweat dripping from his face and neck made him look a mess.

My body shook with silent laughter. *If I don't laugh, I'm going to cry so I might as well laugh.* He looked completely out of his mind, and I didn't care.

"Shut up, Miguel," Beatrice yelled from their bedroom. "She's probably eating the food I got her. Get back in here."

"You better be down there, girl—or else." He staggered back to their room, slamming the door behind him.

Making my way back down the cellar stairs, I allowed myself a smile. The one positive of being scared out of my mind was seeing my so-called father acting like a maniac. No doubt Miguel's boss would have a few things to say to him when he showed up for work later this morning—if he cared to show up at all. Miguel had been sacked from so many jobs, I'd lost count. It forced Beatrice to work for everything they had.

Listening to the silence helped my thoughts start to settle. I stretched out on the settee and fell asleep.

I awake to find Miguel touching my naked shoulder. Somehow he'd removed my clothes while I slept. Pinned on my stomach by his naked body, I'm unable to move. "Miguel? Wh…what?" I gasped, the aroma of alcohol and cocaine registering in my foggy thoughts.

"Shhh, don't say a word," he whispered. His rough fingers traced my face, wiping the hot tears starting to fall. "You're beautiful, baby." His hand moved lower.

"Wh…no." I reached for his hand, but he slapped mine away.

Why? I was asleep! I thought I was done this week. Beatrice, wake up. Lord, help me! Oh no.

My stomach lurched and I had to throw my hand over my mouth to stop the rising pizza from coming out. If I threw up now it would be the end of me. I turned my head away and just let him finish.

"Can I put my clothes back on? It's freezing down here," I whispered, shivering in the dimly lit room.

"Just one more kiss," he said, turning me over.

"No more, please. I'm really tired and—"

Placing a firm hand over my mouth, he glared at me. "Shhh, do what I say or I'll shove the bottle inside of you and let you die here."

I tried to stifle my sob, sniffing a few times, but the tears continued to fall. Finally, I pressed my lips to his. Disobeying him would only get me hit. His hands caressed my back, trapped in his embrace until he sits up.

I reached for my clothes, his eyes looking up and down my slender frame as I dressed. Sighing, I rested my head in my hands and looked at the floor. My thoughts all over the place.

What do I do now? He's not going to stop this. Why didn't you fight harder, Alice? Good Lord, you've let him do this to you how many times? Stand up for yourself!

"Well, thanks for that. I should do this to you more often. You're more cooperative when you're asleep. Good night, baby," Miguel said, walking toward the stairs. Stopping, he quickly walked back to me and cleared his throat.

I looked up into his dark eyes, brewing like storm clouds. He bent his bright red face down toward mine, putting his hands on the back of my head so I couldn't turn away.

"Don't you dare tell a soul about tonight, not even your dear mother." His low and gruff voice sent a chill down my spine.

I laughed and he slapped me across the face.

"Cut the attitude, Alice. Don't tell your mother or anyone else. Consider this your warning. If I find out you've told someone about tonight, I will kill you. Do you understand?" He spat and picked up the bottle. He threw the bottle to the concrete where it shattered, sending splinters of glass across the concrete.

His hands moved to my shoulders, and he shook me. "Do you understand me?"

"Ye...yes, I do." I stammered, my racing heart unable to get anything else out.

Miguel nodded and smiled, seeing he had succeeded in scaring me. "Good, get some rest, you have to go to Edgington in a few hours. I'm so glad to be away from the bloody educational system, myself. It was a nightmare." His offered slight smile made a broken laugh escape out of me, though my hands remained clenched on my knees.

Thankfully, Miguel's expression softened more. Pulling me to my feet, he held me tightly and pressed his lips to mine once more. His fingers running through my hair made the pizza want to come back up again.

"Well, good night, then." He dropped his hands and ascended the stairs.

Listening to his retreating footsteps sent my head spinning. This was the first time he had ever attacked me when I didn't know about it. And I vowed it would be the last.

CHAPTER 2

Chris propped his wide shoulders against the cinnamon-coloured bricks in the main corridor of Edgington College. The steaming Styrofoam cup of coffee warmed his palm, wafting mocha decadence toward his nose. He pursed his lips at the mobile in his other hand. The warning school bell jangled above him, making him jerk but he managed to keep the coffee in its cup.

"Twenty minutes," he mumbled under his breath, glancing at the clock on his mobile.

Mr. Spencer tapped his thick-soled shoes, propping open one of the auditorium doors where choir music drifted through the air.

He read the text one more time, lines creasing his brows. Sighing, he jammed the mobile in his back pocket and slung his backpack over one shoulder. "You've got to be kidding me, Aaliyah. You walked out on the family nine years ago, and now you want to come back into our lives. Yeah right, bitch."

Paper-edged coffee first thing in the morning tasted like honey and chocolate. Chris groaned at the kiss of the hot liquid caressing his tongue and suckling his throat. The bitter words spit at his estranged mother, glass and vinegar moments before, were lost in the rich aroma and silken liquid.

The sound of chattering girls coming closer turned his eyes over his right shoulder.

Images of the mother he hadn't seen since he was nine-years-old vanished in the tangle of long legs and red lips, his favourite kind of woman. Keeping the cup at his lips, he pretended to drink while glancing down at his black slacks, white dress shirt, and black tie. Rolling his eyes, Chris bit the edge of his cup as if he could change his bland uniform into modern fashion with the sheer force of his teeth. It wasn't the most attractive clothing, but at least every boy at Edgington had to dress in the same attire.

Coffee trickled past his tongue making him gasp. The quick inhale drew in even more liquid. He clenched his jaw and forced the pool of lava past his esophagus and into his stomach, though that still didn't save his blistering lips from a choking cough.

His approaching friend, Kariann, walked along with two other girls. Yeah, not just one, but two. Kariann, his best mate, D.J. LePaige's twin sister, chatted on as if she were re-alphabetizing the phone book. Lisi laughed, but the other one, the one he didn't know, only pinched her candy floss lips into a slight smile.

It was the same girl he had seen the other day with Lisi at the girl's swim team practice. He had dragged Luke Clinthill to watch with him so it wouldn't seem too creepy while ensconced in the crowded practice. Her long, powerful legs had sliced through the water, stroking and kicking her way past the other girls to raise herself out of the water and discard her swim cap. He had to push his jaw back into place at her amazing form, his thoughts running wild.

She's fast… She's cute… Why haven't we met? What's her name?

His memory of that day evaporated as fast as the steam from his coffee when her sultry laughter floated to his ears. Golden specks flashed against muddy green eyes, but she dropped her gaze when Chris stared into their hazel depths.

"Christopher, you all right?" Kariann said with a smile.

"Uh yes—" He cleared his throat. "So, who's your friend?" He ran a hand through his strawberry-blonde hair.

Lisi flashed one of her signature smiles, light dancing from her white teeth adding sparkle to the dingy corridor. "This is Alice. Alice, this is Christopher Roblanch. Remember, we saw him and Luke at the swim team practice the other day?"

"Oh yes, I remember seeing you guys. Nice to meet you, Chris."
He nodded at the emerald shards in her eyes.

She brushed back her short, dark curls and traced his features. Her candy floss lips lifted into a lopsided grin when he let the edges of his mouth crease his cheeks.

Wow, Alice, you're really cute. I'm going to make you mine, but how?

"Alice sings, writes lyrics, and plays the drums. She's agreed to be in our band!" Lisi wrapped an arm around Alice's slender shoulders and grinned up at Chris.

Thundering footsteps came toward them.

"Ooo, there's Luke." Lisi dropped her arm and ran down the corridor to meet the tall red-headed boy running toward them— his arms outstretched to hold her.

"Kariann...there you are. Come on. We've got to practice our drama scene again," D.J. said, briskly walking up to the trio. "Hey, Alice."

Alice looked up and nodded, a half smile on her lips.

"Oh, that's right, sorry, Deej," Kariann lengthened the sound of his name in a teasing tone.

"Hey, Chris. How's it going mate? I see you've met Alice. She's a lovely girl." D.J. smiled down at Alice.

She only gave him half a smile, keeping her fingers wrapped tightly around her mobile.

"We better go. See you guys." D.J. called over his shoulder, hurrying away with Kariann.

"See you," Alice and Chris said at the same time and laughed.

"Did you enjoy the swim practice?" Alice barely met his gaze, fidgeting with the mobile in her hands.

"Yeah, girl, you're fast. You look great, too." Chris lifted the coffee cup to his lips and took a drink.

A blush of red climb from Alice's neck all the way up her face. Wiping her brow, she dropped her eyes to the floor. "Oh, well, thanks… That's nice of you to say." She shifted her weight from foot to foot.

"So, Lisi's convinced you to be in her band, that's exciting." Chris's quick glance away caught Luke and Lisi snogging. "Ugh they need to stop that. It's getting on my nerves."

A chuckle bubbled from her lips and a slight smile crept at one corner of her mouth. "Yeah, Lisi is always texting him. It drives her mum crazy."

He used the excuse of a long drink to gaze one more time into her eyes. "Alice, we've been attending Edgington for nearly a year now. Why haven't we met before?"

"Oh…" Her face coloured red again. Drops of sweat dripped from the mobile in her white-knuckled grip. "I keep to myself." She wiped her hands on the hem of her shirt and then ran a hand through her curls.

Chris nodded, imagining himself running her curly strands through his own fingers. Alice's ringing mobile interrupted his thoughts.

She looked down and frowned. He could have sworn he caught a flicker of fear or maybe anger in her eyes before she muted the mobile.

Alice drew the backpack she had slung over one shoulder down into her hand. She yanked open the top, threw the mobile inside, and quickly zipped it shut. "It's my mum." She rolled her eyes and frowned at him.

"Ah, I know how that is," he said with a chuckle, watching her sling her backpack over her shoulder again. "So…since those two—" He gestured to Lisi and Luke who had their heads together looking at a mobile, "—are busy, would you like to take a walk?" The blood thundering through his ears, like a herd of zebra stampeding in his brain, muted out her reply, but he did see a head nod.

They ventured off down the corridor and outside onto Edgington's grounds, walking along a gray stone pathway, which meandered by Edgington's greenhouse and football pitch. Beneath tall, leafy trees, streams of sunlight danced along the path in a duet with the shadows.

"So, Alice, where do you live?" he said, wrapping both hands around the coffee cup.

Biting her bottom lip, she frowned and turned her head away from his gaze. With quickened steps, she walked away from him and his question. Turning back to him, she kept her expression neutral, but Chris noticed a new quick rise and fall to her chest.

"I live with Lisi, most of the time. The rest of the time, I'm forced to live with my mum and step-father." She made a quick rub at the eyelashes surrounding her right eye. "What about you?"

"I live with my dad, Hugh, younger sister, Kanene, step-mum, Tara and her three kids…Kenneth, Gavin, Emmalyn. And they have a baby together…Erin. It's loud in the house, but it's fine," Chris said, watching her chest begin to slow, rising and falling at an even pace once more.

"I see…" She nodded and unfolded her hands, wiping the sweat on her denim, knee-length skirt. "I'm the only child in the house." The gleaming white smile she flashed him almost disarmed every thought in his head. "Sometimes, I wish there were other children in the house. You're lucky."

He chuckled. "Yeah, I suppose."

He walked along beside her, listening to the sounds of birds chirping, the trees fluttering in the slight breeze, and faint shouts of fellow students calling to one another. Chris was about to ask another question when her mobile vibrated against the books in her pack. She paid no attention to it and continued walking.

"We should probably start heading back," she said with a slight smile.

"Uh, yes." He nodded, looking down at her, lost in his thoughts. *Hmm, perhaps Alice and her mum had a row this morning and Alice doesn't want to talk to her.*

They made their way back to Edgington in silence, the scent of warm vanilla drifting along the breeze from her sun-kissed skin.

***

Chris's focus only grew worse as the day dragged on. In calculus, he wrote Alice's name in the margins of his notebook. In chemistry, she sat at the desk to his right. Chris hunched over his book and tried again to concentrate, but the smell of vanilla intruded his thoughts. In football practice, he kept hearing her voice. The distraction threw his entire game off. When the final bell rang, Chris ran through the corridors to the car park.

"Hey Chris, where are you off to?" D.J. yelled, running to meet him.

To find some sanity. Chris rolled his eyes and turned to his friend. "Oh, I have a family play date at the park. Should be fun, I guess. That Alice girl is really cute, mate." Holding his mobile, he swiped to his text messages and started to type one.

"Yeah, she's really nice. You should have a real chat with her sometime." D.J.'s blue eyes sparkled and his face lifted into a smile when a van pulled up beside them.

"Yeah, maybe. Well, I better go." Chris grinned at his father, who wound down the window.

"Hey, D.J., good to see you again. Come on, Chris." His father started to bang on the steering wheel, singing to a British, classic rock song about having the bloody right to speak.

"Right. Uh...see you mate," Chris said, slapping D.J. on the back. He hurried to climb in the back of the van.

"Hi, Hugh, Tara, great to see you again. I'll call you about the cinema and text you Alice's number. See you later!" D.J. gave Chris and his family a wave and walked toward Edgington.

Chris sat in the back of the van listening to Tara and his father sing along to the old man's favourite music. He rolled his eyes and grimaced when their hands in the middle intertwined. His father turned up the volume on the stereo and they belted out another song.

Why would you reference finding a girl to a wolf hunt? It's so bizarre, but it makes sense...the work of a poet, which I am not.

At the park, Tara got out of the car and started unloading the five younger children. His father had one leg out of the van when a song by the most famous British, classic rock quartet came on. Turning up the volume, his father sang the lyrics, oblivious to Tara struggling to keep the children by the van and get the baby out of the car seat.

"Hugh, I know you love this song, but I really need your help. I only have two hands, love. I can't get the other bags, too."

His father slid out of the van with a sincere apology written on his face, but Tara still muttered under her breath. Shaking her head, she frowned at Chris who had returned to the van with two little girls clinging to his hands. Instead of comment, Tara lifted the nappy rucksack on her back and took the baby out of the car seat.

Chapter 3

Edgington College had wealth running throughout its corridors. Lisi belonged to that crowd, and since she gave me everything I didn't have, it ensured I fit right in along with her. It was an inside joke between us, that the star of the swim team had hardly anything to her name, because her drug addicted parents took everything for themselves and constantly kicked her out of the house. I attended Edgington for free because of my family's low income. Without Lisi, I would have been a disgrace and looked down upon by my peers. Instead, they liked me and considered me one of their own.

However, I kept to myself as much as possible. The worst thing that could happen was someone finding out about where I lived. Everytime anyone asked, I became Lisi's foster sister, which was true and much better than outing my deepest secret—being the daughter of a drug addicted maniac.

Hurrying to the changing rooms, I was caught in the corridor by Chris.

"You all right, Alice?" Chris leaned against the cinnamon-coloured brick wall.

"Yeah, are you all right?" I folded my hands together and forced myself to look up at his broad smile.

"Yeah, thanks! Do you want to talk to Luke and me at lunch about the band? We can start showing you what we're doing." His frantic fingers tapped and swiped on his mobile.

"Oh sure, I'm excited." I gave him a slight smile.

"Cool. Do you think we could—"

Lisi and Kariann came walking up, chatting about something. Looking past his shoulder at them, Chris's eyes narrowed and a frown dragged his face down.

"Alice, I'll see you at the pool," Kariann said with a smile.

I nodded, returning the friendly gesture to both girls. "What did you want, Chris?"

Sighing, Chris lowered his mobile and looked down at me through his eyelashes. "Oh, it was nothing. I need to go. I'll see you in chemistry."

"Okay, see you then," I said, giving him a quick smile.

He gave a nod and I turned away. Lisi caught me by the arm.

"Lisi, I need to go." I flattened my lips. I didn't have time for her teasing right now.

"Sorry, he's a really nice guy. I think he likes you. You should give him a chance," she said, glancing in Chris's direction.

I shook my head.

"Alice, what's going on? You didn't answer my text last night." She stepped toward me, her hands clenched together in a white-knuckle grip.

Shrugging, I stepped toward the wall to let a group of boys and girls pass by. "I know. Sorry, Lisi, I've been dealing with a lot, and it slipped my mind." I wasn't sure if I trusted Lisi enough to explain what I was dealing with at the hands of my step-father. But the way Lisi's eyes narrowed, I had to give her something—even if only the partial truth. "I had to stay with Beatrice's sister, Lindsie."

Frowning, she sighed. "Don't tell me, Beatrice kicked you out again."

I nodded and she groaned. "I'm sorry. Did you tell Lindsie anything?"

Her mobile vibrated in her pack and she pulled it out and replied to a text message.

"Of course not! Lisi, I need you to listen to me," I said, my voice low and quiet.

Nodding, she finished the text and darkened her mobile. Stepping closer, she looked at me, her eyes never leaving my gaze.

"I can't take it anymore. Beatrice and Miguel are going to kill me if I don't get out of there. You don't know what they do to me, Lisi. I can't handle the— Are you texting Luke?" I narrowed my eyes, looking at her typing frantically on her mobile.

"Alice, I—well I." She turned away, looking over her shoulder at Luke who was coming toward us.

Stopping, he had a word with Chris.

I sighed and glared at her. "Kahleesi, give me your attention for two seconds, please. I need to stay with you and your family, permanently. I have nowhere else to go. I need information about my dad, and I have something that I bet your mum will know about." My heart thundered in my chest. My clenched fists longed for something to beat on. I focused on my breathing to cool the anger surging through my body.

Lisi's dark green eyes widened and her mouth fell open. I knew I had her attention when she fidgeted with her light brown hair. "Alice, how could my mum help with your dad?" Lisi let Luke take her hand. "After Edgington we'll go to my house and find out what she knows, all right?"

I nodded, giving both of them a quick goodbye as they walked away.

I changed into a light-blue swimsuit, with a matching swim cap, and black swim goggles for my first and favourite lesson of the day—swimming.

Miss Kai, head swim coach, gave me a warm smile when I approached the pool. Lean and thin as a rail, Miss Kai stood at the water's edge with her mobile in hand, ready to time my warmup drills. She looked like a supermodel pretending to pose for invisible photographers in her white bikini.

"Hello Alice! Good to see you. Looking a bit knackered?"

"Yeah, I was up early this morning, doing homework again." I watched her push a strand of curly, red hair behind her ear. "You know, just like last week." I offered a slight smile.

She shook her head, frowning. "Come on Alice, you're the best on the team. You've got to get more rest. You're going to kill yourself." She readied her mobile and I gave a slight nod. I took my place at the blocks, reaching down to dive in. "All right, in three, two, one."

Without hesitation, I dove into the pool and began swimming warm up drills. After completing the warm up drills, I practiced my 200-meter Individual Medley. Beginning with the butterfly, then on to backstroke and breaststroke, I finished with freestyle where I worked on my crawl technique.

The exhilaration of forcing my body to work hard, pushed the effects from lack of sleep away. Swimming was the one place where I could be who I wanted to be, and forget the hell of my messed up home life. Practicing five days a week, with swim competitions every weekend, kept me in good form, and made me strive to be better at my craft.

As if swimming was not enough, I filled my schedule with as many A-Level courses I could manage. I was determined to get into university and become a swim coach. I liked working with kids and wanted to show them that they could accomplish hard things, if they set their minds to it.

I watched my teammates practice their drills with pride. Edgington College was on its way to win the first-ever cup in the United Kingdom College Championship Autumn Swim Gala at the end of the term. Changing into my Edgington uniform, a white blouse with a black, lacey collar, and black cuffs on the sleeves with a knee-length denim skirt, I wondered about my father… My real father, not the maniac at home who waited there to take advantage of me. I came from someone else—I clung to that hope with every fiber of my being. I vowed to learn the truth of my origin, no matter what it cost. Hiding from my home life was getting harder each day. Something had to give or I would have a nervous breakdown, and my life would fall apart.

Bowing my head to hide my tears, I clenched my hands together. The tears fell hot and fast down my cheeks as I whispered a frantic prayer. "Lord, give me the strength to keep it together another day. I can't take it anymore. Please let me get away from this hell." I dabbed at my eyes with a tissue, my pulse slowing.

Walking into the corridor, I kept my head low, giving slight nods to my peers and mumbling soft hellos. The constant pretense of being outwardly happy was wearing on me. I was relieved to enter my second lesson, chemistry with Mr. Brody. Chris sat next to me, but neither of us spoke. We were too busy frantically taking notes, though I caught Chris staring at me a couple of times.

Later, in Edgington's canteen, I sat with Chris, Luke, and Lisi, eating our meals of roast chicken and potatoes. Luke had written a ballad for the band on a pad of paper that we all looked over. I mentioned a couple of changes, which everyone liked. Chris and Luke came up with melodies for guitar and bass and explained what songs I would drum, sing, or drum and sing on.

Later that evening, when we finished our first band practice, Lisi and I made our way to Lisi's house. Lisi remained unusually quiet on the drive.

"Lisi, are you all right?" I said glancing at her and back out the windscreen.

"Oh yeah, I'm terrific. Hey, Alice, do you know what your real father's name is?"

I smiled and shook my head, wiping my sweaty palms on my skirt. "I told you... Beatrice won't tell me a thing. She keeps insisting Miguel's my father." Lisi cringed at the same time I did. "I'm not going to get anything out of her." I retrieved the drumsticks that rolled off my legs and landed on the floorboard. "You know how stubborn she can be—the bitch."

We laughed as Lisi pulled the car into the driveway.

When she parked the car, I looked into her green eyes. "Lisi, do you think your mum knows who my father is?" If she didn't, I had no idea where to look next.

CHAPTER 4

Chris bounced the ball off his trainer but stopped when he heard his father yell.

"Chris, you could have that ball juggled a dozen more times if you'd focus on the ball instead of your mother's stupidity."

"What?" Why bring her up now? Chris's feet dragged across the grass until the ball rolled onto his shin, and then back down until it rocked beside his feet.

Sitting on the grass, Chris folded his hands together on his knees and looked up at the motionless tree branches. Chris's mind thought back to one of his favourite memories with the woman he once called mother—sitting at the picnic table in the back-garden, finger-painting with chocolate mousse.

He could see the mess of moose on his paper and all over his clothes. He watched his mother take a finger full of chocolate mousse from the white porcelain bowl in front of her to paint chocolate, puffy clouds. He watched her manicured hand with red-polished nails paint the border of the clouds and fill them in with more moose. He smelled the chocolate and watched her take a finger of moose and write his name on his cheek. He tried to write her name but was unsuccessful, getting the letters "i" and "y" in reverse order. Frowning in dismay, his eyes burned with unshed tears.

"It's all right honey, you'll get it. Look how close you are to getting the letters right. I'm so proud of you, Chris," she said, gazing down at him. Her blue eyes sparkled along with her white smile.

"Thanks." He grinned at her.

"Oh my! Look at you, sweetie. We need to wash you up. But first…" Her grin grew even broader. "You're going to get messier, Chris!" She spread a handful of cold, chocolate mousse on his face.

Chris could still hear the jubilant laughter from his mother and himself when they started throwing moose at each other. He watched her jump up from the table and run around the lawn trying to avoid his chocolate mousse attack.

"Oh no, you got me, son!" She bent down for him to slather moose all over her face and clothes. She then pulled out the hosepipe and sprayed their clothes, which started a water fight. The bowls containing the chocolate mousse were washed and used to pour water on each other. She squealed with delight, laughing right along with him while they saturated themselves.

* * *

Chris sat with his father, Hugh, on the settee. Game controllers in their hands, the video game Monster Knights played on the television screen. They entered level five and his father smiled at him.

"All right, Chris, let's help protect Covendom Kingdom."

Chris nodded, a broad smile on his face. His eyes scanned the screen before resting on his father's face, his eyes the same matching blue-gray shade as his own. "Yeah, this is going to be great."

His father's video character ran left then right, trying to avoid the many knights in golden armor advancing toward his silver armor-clad knight. "Ahh, come on then. Help me, Chris. What the—"

Chris chuckled and brandished his sword on the screen, vanquishing the golden-armored knights. "Ahh, there's more of them? Oh no, they're blocking me in a corner. Get back, you. Ugh, I can't get out."

"Oh no, son, I'm coming for you. Get back, you thieving heathens. Get back, I'm not going to let you take my son or Covendom." His father hit a golden knight with his sword.

"Oh wait, there's a secret door." Chris used his video character to tap his armor-clad hand along different stones in the brown stone wall blocking him on two sides.

His father's character kept waving his sword at a furious rate, making the golden knights scatter. "I say, Chris, they're coming after me. Ahh, where did you go? Hey, oh no...now I'm in the moat." His father frowned, waiting for his screen to refresh.

Chris went through the stone wall and climbed a matching stone staircase to the roof of the castle. He dodged winged horses carrying golden knights that threw daggers. "I'm on top of the castle. Ugh, there's one golden knight who won't give up...Knock it off you—"

"So, Chris, how's football?" On screen his father fought the golden knights again, making his way to the corner that Chris had just left.

"It's fine."

"Good. Chris, I think we need to talk about—"

"Dad, hang on, I'm just about to go into the dragon's pen and—"

"Christopher, we need to talk." His father placed a hand on his arm.

Sighing, Chris paused the game and set his game controller next to him. "Dad, I really don't want to talk about mum."

"I know you don't want to talk about her son, but it's time. You know, sometimes, adults say and do stupid things when they're angry. I don't know what sort of rubbish Aaliyah said to you before she left, but she wasn't right in the head."

"She never said anything to me. Did she say something to you? Did she blame this on me?"

"No, your mum sometimes got very angry and she didn't think about what she said in the heat of the moment."

"What are you talking about? I don't understand." Chris glared into his father's blue-gray eyes.

"I know, son. I want to make sure you're okay. I worry she put all sorts of rubbish into your head."

Heat rose into Chris's face. He clenched his hands on his knees into fists. "Dad, I didn't mean to let her down. I didn't mean to chase her off. I didn't mean to eat the biscuits, or spill the bubbles on the floor. It was an accident. I didn't mean to yell at Kanene. She played with my toys and I didn't like it. I didn't mean to get bad grades, or forget to do my chores."

His father's hand touched his shoulder. "Christopher, I'm not blaming you son. I—"

"It doesn't matter. Aaliyah never even told me goodbye! She ran off one day when I was at school. She didn't say a bloody word." There he said it—ripping his heart open all over again. He hated the tears pouring down his cheeks.

"No, no, Chris, I..." His father looked as comfortable with the confession as he felt foolish, picking up the game controller and pushing buttons. But since he'd opened this can of worms, Chris wanted it all off his chest.

"She left me behind because I wasn't good enough for her. I always did everything wrong in her eyes. I never behaved well enough. It's my bloody fault Aaliyah left us. She couldn't wait to get away from me." Not that his father would ever understand, he had never been bloody abandoned.

"Tara, are you and the children back, love?" His father dropped the game controller and rose to his feet. "I thought I heard her in the kitchen."

Oh now his father wanted to run away? He should have just left the subject alone in the first place. He never wanted to see her again. "I hate the lot of you!" Chris shouted, rising to his feet. He ran into the kitchen, past the open door, and the jovial chatter coming from his younger siblings.

His father followed after him. "Chris, I—"

"Leave me alone," Chris said, running down the cellar stairs.

He collapsed onto his bed and buried his face into his pillow. A hand started rubbing his back, but he refused to acknowledge it. His body shook and his breaths came fast, the tears flowing freely onto his pillow.

"Son, I had no idea you were having such a hard time. And, I'm sorry for all of it. Can I explain what happened?"

Chris didn't feel like responding.

"Chris, I think it's best if I—"

"Shut it," he said, lifting his tear stained face to glare up at his father. "Just leave me alone."

"Chris, we can sort this out if we—"

"Get out." He shouted.

His father's shoulders slumped but he did as he demanded, taking his hand off Chris's back and walking out of the room.

Overhead, the faint voices of Tara and Hugh conversed. At hearing the children running down the cellar stairs, Chris groaned.

"No, leave me alone, the lot of you," he muttered, getting off the bed and walking toward his door.

"Chris, what's the matter?" His sister Emmalyn stopped in her tracks, staring at his wet face.

"Emmy dear, leave Chris alone. Let's go get a snack," Tara said, herding the children back up the stairs. Chris listened to them run into the kitchen with their happy exclamations to his father, telling him about their fun at the park.

Tara's smile evaporated when she turned her eyes upon Chris. "Your dad told me what happened between you two. I'm so sorry—"

"Can we please just drop it." Chris leaned against the door frame, wishing he could be anywhere but here.

"Why don't you take some time for yourself and come join

us for some fresh air when you're ready? The boys want to learn some football from you and your dad." She smiled but Chris still shook his head. "All right then." She walked up a couple of steps, but turned around. "We love you, son," she said before leaving.

Sighing, Chris shut the door and walked over to his bed. That was the last thing he wanted to hear right now. Glancing at his mobile sitting on the bedside table, he noticed a notification—a text message from an unknown number.

If the message was from Aaliyah he might chuck the mobile across the room. Maybe it was the only way to stop her from intruding in his life. Typing in the password, Chris sniffed and wiped at tears leaking from his eyes.

Chris's heart raced when he read who it was from.

Hey, Chris, it's Alice. Lisi gave me your number and told me to text you. It's been nice talking with you the last few days.

"Yes!" Chris said, a smile lifting his face. "Who cares about my family drama—Alice just text me." He read her message again. "Alice, somehow, I will make you mine."

He tapped a reply, picked up his car keys and ran up the cellar stairs. He ran out the front door without a word to his parents, jumped in the car and sped away. Blasting his favourite songs, he drove to Edgington, where Alice waited.

CHAPTER 5

Sitting across from me at the kitchen table, I locked eyes with Krisany, Lisi's mother, for a split second. She clenched her hands together, her eyes darting from me to the papers in front of me and to the clock over my head.

"Here's the letters, Krissy." I slid them over to her.

With hands shaking, she took the papers and read the letters. When she finished, she shook her head and looked at me with misty eyes. "It upsets me that you had to discover Jack this way, Alice. It wasn't right of Beatrice to..." She sighed and glared at the papers. "Beatrice is despicable! I'm going to get the results of that paternity test right now."

I jumped out of my seat, the blood draining from my face. "Don't tell her I did this—she'll have Miguel on me in no time."

Krisany smiled and motioned for me to sit down. I obeyed but with great trepidation, watching her unlock her mobile and tap on Beatrice's number.

After one ring, Beatrice's over-excited voice rang out. "Krissy, darling, how are you?"

I frowned, she only had that voice for her friends, I never heard it.

"I'm terrific. Thanks, love. Don't worry, I'm not ringing you about Alice, she's fine. Do you remember the paternity test Jack Julian took when Alice was a baby? Do you have the results? Alice is asking about her father again and I need to settle the matter once and for all—"

"Of course I do," Beatrice said, her voice ringing out over the speaker. "The paper's in a safety deposit box in my wardrobe. I keep the key with me at all times. I know Alice would be all over it if she could get into it. I can't let you have it—Alice will find out—"

"Beatrice, listen, I only have fifteen minutes. Alice and Lisi went to pick out new lipstick at the Coral Clover. I need to get that paper so I can burn it. That will shut Alice up."

Beatrice sighed loudly. "I'm so sorry. I told you she wouldn't shut up about her father."

I smirked with a nod. "If you only have a few minutes, you'd better get over here. You're so sweet looking out for me and keeping my secret safe, Krissy, darling."

Krisany's smile widened with her response. "Great! I'll be right over to get it from you. See you soon."

"Okay, love. Sounds good," Beatrice said.

Hanging up the mobile we jumped up, elated. Krisany pulled me into her arms.

"How did you do that without yelling at her?" I said.

"I can manage around her because I know she's a nightmare. She's more agreeable when Miguel's not around, eh?"

I frowned. "I've never seen that side of her. He's always around and I'm always in trouble with both of them. I'm going to read a book." I walked to the staircase. Reaching the first step, Krisany called to me.

"Alice, whatever the results of this test are, know that I'll always be here for you."

I nodded and gave a sincere thank you before turning around and walking up the stairs.

My heart raced with the thought of someone other than Miguel being my father. I picked up David Copperfield, but finding concentration was impossible. Placing the book back on the bookshelf, my thoughts landed on Jack. I tried to imagine what his life has been like.

Jack knows there's a possibility he could have a baby, but he has no idea what came of the test. If he is my real father, will he remember what happened between him and Beatrice? Will he want anything to do with me? Is he married? Does he have any other children? When I meet him, will he like me? Will he want a relationship with me? What if we don't get along? What if the test results say Miguel Esposito is my real father? What will I do then?

I didn't let the thought of Miguel being my father continue for fear of losing my lunch. I walked back downstairs and sat on the settee to wait. At the sound of Krisany's car pulling up, my heart threatened to jump out of my chest. Waiting for her to come inside seemed like an eternity.

She handed me an envelope with a smile. "I have no idea what the results are. Beatrice says hello." She sat down next to me.

With shaking hands, I opened the envelope and pulled out the document. Knowing about my past could only help my future. After a deep breath, I read the results. My eyes filled with tears, making everything blurry. Blinking, I reread the results.

"Jack Julian is my father."

Reading the results for the fifth time, I heard someone sobbing. I thought it was Krisany but soon realized the sound came from me.

"How could Beatrice keep me from this?" I screamed. "I hate her! She's tortured me for my entire life. It's not fair! She can't keep doing this to me. I have a dad." I stood, unable to bear the suddenly stuffy room. "Krissy, I need to get out of here."

"I understand. Where would you like to go?"

"Take me to Edgington. I need to swim some laps." I ran upstairs to collect my swimming gear.

Krisany didn't say a word while speeding toward Edgington. I held the test results in a white-knuckled grip until she pulled into Edgington's car park. I handed her the paper with a quick thank you and ran inside.

I barely nodded to the peers saying hello to me, scurrying to the changing rooms.

I threw on my swimming gear and dove into the pool. Swimming laps calmed my thundering heart. The smile on my face seemed to grow wider with every lap I made down the pool. Nothing could ruin my happiness.

CHAPTER 6

Running into the main corridor of Edgington, Chris met D.J. and Kariann. "Have you seen Luke or Lisi?"

Kariann smiled up at him. "Yes, they're by the changing rooms."

"Terrific, do you know if Alice happened to be with them?"

"I don't know, you might try—"

Turning away with a wave, Chris ran down the corridor to the changing rooms. Luke and Lisi stood outside, locked in an embrace.

Chris panted, running up to them. "Have you seen Alice?"

"Yeah, she's practicing her drills. What's the rush?" Luke's corny smile left Chris wondering why he even bothered asking.

"I need to talk to her." Chris ran a hand through his hair.

"All right, I'm sure she'll be done soon. She's been in there for over an hour," Lisi said. "She's really improving on her butterfly kick."

Luke nodded.

"Should I go to the pool, or—"

The changing room doors opened to the right of the trio. Alice walked out, her wet, curly hair falling across her bare shoulders. The white tank top she wore highlighted her sun-kissed skin.

"Hey, Alice, I'm so glad I found you." Chris smiled down at her but she looked away.

Shaking her head she stepped passed the group.

"Alice, I—" He noticed four, faded yellow and brown marks

across her left bicep. "Hey, wait up. You've done something to your arm." Catching up to her, he ran his fingers along the bruise. "What happened?"

Alice slung her backpack off and threw it into Chris's abdomen. "Ouch, what was that—"

"Shhh, stop asking questions. I'll tell you, but not here." She gestured around the corridor where a few groups of students lingered.

Chris thinned his lips into a flat line and narrowed his eyes, but could understand not wanting to air personal issues to just anyone. He had plenty of his own. "All right then, let's go." Glancing behind him, he saw Luke and Lisi chatting with D.J. and Kariann. "Well, they're busy so—"

Alice hit him again.

"Ouch."

"I told you to shut up. I'll explain everything in a moment. Let's go, and not another word from you." She had her hands clenched around the backpack strap like she might take another swing.

He held up his hands and followed after her.

Alice stopped a good distance away from Edgington, near a grove of trees. "My arm was an accident. I fell and my step-father helped me up."

"It doesn't look like that kind of a mark, Alice." Chris traced the marks on her arm. "It looks like he intentionally hurt you. What's going on?"

Alice's expression flickered from anger to fear in seconds. "I already told you, my step-father was helping me up." She smiled like it wasn't that big of a deal. He refused to let such a beautiful smile distract him.

"It doesn't look that way to me, and I'm concerned." Chris bent, wanting a closer examination of her eyes.

She bit her lower lip and dropped her gaze to the grass, her body shaking. "Alice, what's going on? You're terrified. I can see it in your face."

Without a word, she turned to leave. Instinct had him reaching out to stop her. She flinched at his touch on her shoulder.

"Don't touch me!" She spun around, her hands clenched into fists and her face crimson. With eyes narrowed and lips pursed she glared up at him. "What the hell do you think you're doing?" Her eyes clouded with unshed tears.

"Wait, what? I don't understand." He put his offending hand behind his back.

"Just stop asking questions, please."

"Listen, Alice, if you think this is helping your case, you're mistaken. This is only making me more worried. Look, whatever you tell me I'll keep to myself, all right?"

"And why should I believe you? I barely even know you." She gave a mirthless laugh.

Sighing, Chris edged closer and held her gaze. "I'm sorry, it seems like I'm coming at you really strong, but there's something about you that I can't ignore. I think I like you."

Her mouth fell open and her eyes widened. "What? You're kidding."

Her sudden laughter lightened the mood, making Chris laugh, too.

"I'm not kidding. I think you're cute."

She touched her lips, her face colouring.

"So, could we try dating?"

"Mmm...I suppose, if you want too," she whispered. "I've never had anyone show any interest in me before." Dropping her gaze, she frowned at the ground.

"Are you okay?" Chris reached for her hand but her icy fingers made him jump. "Whoa, your fingers are freezing." He chuckled.

"Sorry, all the blood leaves my fingers when I'm nervous." Her face turned an even darker red.

"That's all right," he said, tightening his grip on her hand. Staring into her dark eyes, a million questions ran through his mind.

What are you all about? Why are you so secretive about your life? Why are you so nervous? Will you let me in?

"You still haven't answered my question." He stepped closer. Frowning, she turned away. "Why do you keep turning away from me?"

Turning back to face him, her eyes brimmed with tears. "I'm sorry, Chris. It's what I do at home. It helps me deal with—" She sniffed, "—with them."

"Who? Your parents?"

At her nod, Chris moved closer. He could smell the mango body butter drifting from her sun-kissed skin. It was all he could do not to kiss her. Gently, he wrapped his arms around her until he felt her stiffen. He pulled back but didn't completely pull away, hoping she would believe she was safe with him. "What do they do to you?" he whispered.

Her body trembled in his arms. Chris lifted her chin, forcing her to look at him. Her bottom lip quivered.

"My parents get drunk and go crazy a lot. If I'm not careful, I get caught in the crossfire of their fights, and my step-father rages at me," she whispered through ragged breaths. Laying her head on his chest she fell to pieces.

"You've got to be kidding me." The reality of her words sunk in, stoking a fire of hatred for a man he'd never met. "How can he do that to you? I ought to kill that son-of-a—"

"No, you can't." She moaned into his shirt.

"Alice, if he's hurting you, we've got to tell some—"

The quick lift of her head and glare stopped him from saying more.

"Chris, promise me you won't tell anyone. You don't understand how dangerous my step-father is. Please, don't tell anyone, or..." A flood of tears poured down her cheeks and her head returned to his chest.

"Or what?" Afraid to do more, Chris patted the tank-top-fabric covering her back.

"He'll kill me." She sobbed. The straps of her backpack slid from her arms, the whole thing dropping to the ground with a thud. Her slender arms wound around his waist.

Her initiation of the action gave Chris the confidence to again try and hold her close. Caressing her back, he struggled with what else he might say or do. No one had ever had such an emotional breakdown in front of him before.

After a few minutes, she started to relax. She lifted her face, gazing her now bloodshot eyes up at him.

"Feel better?" He fingered a loose strand of her hair back behind her ear.

Nodding, she sniffed several times and bent down to retrieve her backpack. She reached into her pack and pulled out a package of tissues. She dabbed at her eyes and cleared her throat. "Yes, I just needed to cry. I've been keeping it a secret for so long, I was close to losing my mind. I guess I don't have to warn you that my life is a bloody mess."

"Are you sure you don't want to tell anyone? We could—"

"No, no. I'll be fine, really. I just needed to talk about it."

He reached around and pressed on her back, to escort her wherever she wanted to go. Her sharp inhale and flinch away had him dropping his hand. "Oh, Lord, I'm sorry. Did I hurt you?"

"It's all right, it's just a bruise."

"Another one? What the hell is happening to you?"

"It's nothing." Her eyes pleaded with him to just let it go, but every warning bell inside him said these weren't signs to be ignored.

"A bruise on your arm and one on your back doesn't seem like nothing."

"I'm fine, Chris. I promise." A half smile played at one of the corners of her lips, but he still wasn't deterred.

"Can I see the bruise on your back then?" He couldn't believe he'd just said that. Under any other circumstances he wouldn't blame her for slapping his face, but she didn't.

She slumped her shoulders and sighed. "Okay."

He followed her behind a nearby bush. Dropping her backpack, she checked for any possible onlookers then turned her back toward him. Impressed by the trust she showed, he made a mental promise not to focus on anything but what he'd asked to see. She lifted her tank top and he didn't even have to gulp back improper thoughts at the sight of her white bra.

Five bruises lined her back. In different stages of healing, two were black and blue, and another yellow and brown, but two of the bruises looked swollen.

"Oh, my, God." He couldn't stop himself from stepping closer to trace the marks on her warm skin. He stopped at the swollen ones. "These look like they hurt the most."

She nodded, her curls moving up and down with her head movement.

"It's like he's trying to kill you." How could any father, even a step-father, do such a thing? He crossed his arms. "How has nobody seen these bruises when you're swimming?"

"I don't talk much at Edgington, and I'm really good at coming up with believable stories. There are a couple bruises on my stomach too."

"Are you serious? And your mother?"

"Does nothing to stop it." She lowered her tank top and bent down to retrieve her backpack from the grass.

"What is wrong with your parents? It's criminal. This shouldn't be happening to you. I'd love to go over there and—"

"Shhh," she said, covering his mouth, "not so loud. I don't want anyone to know. If this were to get back to my step-father, he would kill me. You've seen it on my back. Those are punishments for not doing what he thinks is right."

She pulled her hand away and he couldn't stop himself from continuing. "That's crazy!"

"I know it is." She smiled up at him. "It's just a few more months until I turn eighteen, then I can get the hell away from them…for good." She reached out and squeezed his bicep.

"Yeah, you better."

"Chris…"

He nodded, loving the way she said his name. He could already tell he was going to have a hard time saying no to anything she asked of him.

"Thanks for being cool about all this."

"It makes sense why you don't interact a lot with others." He opened his arms and, this time, it didn't take any coaxing for her to enter. "I'm not okay with it, and you shouldn't be okay with it, either."

She rested her head on his chest, but said nothing.

Her silent nearness played on his heightened senses until he couldn't take it anymore. "Hey, Alice?"

"Yes?" She lifted her head.

Seizing the opportunity, Chris bent and captured her lips with his. Her eyes flew wide but her shaking body didn't pull away, until her mobile chimed with an incoming text from Krisany.

Alice, I hate to break it to you, darling, but we've got an appointment at Wandsworth.

Chris looked down at Alice's mobile. "What's Wandsworth?"

Alice looked up at him and shook her head. "I have no idea, but I'm about to find out."

CHAPTER 7

I climbed into the car with Krisany. She put the key in the ignition and handed me a black book from her handbag.

"What's this?" I traced the leather cover. The book smelled of worn leather and old notepaper.

"It's your father's journal. You need to know what he did to land himself in prison before we meet him this afternoon."

My breathing stopped and my mouth fell open. "We're going to see him, right now?"

"Yes, it's important you know who he is, so I scheduled the appointment. I don't want you to have any other secrets kept from you." Krisany grabbed my hand and squeezed. "I met Jack when Beatrice and I were attending university. Jack was a nice fellow—I had a crush on him at one point." Chuckling, she put the car into motion.

"Oh wow, but, prison?" My stomach flipped at her nod. If he'd known about me, would he still have ended up in prison? "Krissy, how did you get his journal?"

"Jack asked me to keep it for him. He didn't trust that his parents would keep it safe."

The temptation to look inside couldn't be denied. I opened the book. My father's cursive flowed neatly down every page I thumbed through. An entry jumped out at me, making my hands tremble. I squeezed the edges tighter to keep from dropping it.

I'm ashamed to recount everything, but here's how my life went to hell... Andrew Carson was my flatmate at Oxford. I had graduated and found employment doing engineering for a great company. Andrew was finishing up his chemistry major. Andrew and I went to a party with some of our friends. That's where I met Krissy and Beatrice Christi-Ellen Charbel, an attractive blonde, blue-eyed girl, until I saw what she was like after the fact. Dancing, conversing, and many drinks led us to her flat and eventually... her bed. It was my first time. Beatrice admitted she had no idea how many times it was for her. She had lost count. I should have never gone to that party, that was the start of my downfall.

Jack's tone held such despair, that didn't get any better when I flipped to the next page.

The next morning, I woke with a massive headache. What the hell had I done.

I searched the flat for Beatrice and found her snorting cocaine through a straw. A piping hot cup of tea sat on the table next to her. I asked what the hell she was doing, but she was blissfully entranced.

She brushed my comment off and said she was going to meet up with her boyfriend, Miguel Esposito.

"What would you do if you were pregnant?" I said, shocked by what I

saw. *"Would you carry on like this?" I gestured to her hands holding the straw and cocaine packet in a death grip.*

"Of course not, Jack. I'd clean up for the health of my child. Won't you join me?" She looked at me with those big, blue eyes, batting her eyelashes, but I refused to be influenced by her again.

"Hell no. You need to clean up." I walked out without another word or glance.

"So, that's how I came to be. The letters were true," I said to Krisany, tapping the words I just read. She said nothing, but when I glanced at her she was focused on the road. I shrugged my shoulders and turned the page.

Today, I bought a new car. I've had my eye on it for a while now. It's a black SUV. It has sleek lines, leather interior. It's fast, and I love it. It took a lot of money, but I'm so excited to be done with my old car that was falling apart. Now I'm sitting on fine leather seats.

I gave Jenny and her husband a ride, cruising down the motorway blasting our favourite songs. It made me happy.

"He likes fancy cars too," I said with a smile. "What happened, Jack?" I glanced out the windscreen.

I turned a few more pages, trying to discover Jack's crime. In my skimming, only one name popped out—Andrew Carson—but I had to stop. Nausea from the motion of the car hit me, giving me a massive headache and cold sweats.

Not long after, we reached Wandsworth Prison. My heart pounded, being led inside by Krisany to white, plastic chairs. The smell of tobacco and sweat reminded me of Beatrice's house, making my stomach turn all over again. Sitting there, I shuffled my feet and clenched my hands against the icy sensation slithering from my hair and down my neck like the tongues of snakes. Staring at the watch on my wrist only made my anxiety grow. The hands seemed to be dragging through thicker and thicker sand the longer we sat here. And why did shackled men have to keep passing in front of us?

I don't think I can do this. Maybe I should run? My stomach is killing me. Do I really want to know who this man, my father, is? Wait. Yes, I do. Anyone would be better than Miguel.

At last, a stern-faced guard with a name tag "Hatman" called Krisany's name. I followed her on shaking legs.

Led into a small room with gray, stone walls, a small, brown desk sat in the center with three white, plastic chairs. Krisany sat down and motioned for me to sit next to her. I shook my head. My dry mouth couldn't form words. Instead, I leaned against the cool, stone wall. The knots twisting my stomach made me want to vomit. The thought of meeting a stranger and dropping this bomb on him terrified me.

Would he love me or would he want nothing to do with me? Maybe he would hate knowing he had a daughter. Would he accept me?

My mind spun like the reel of a film. My eyes burned with unshed tears at the thought of someone else rejecting me, yet, somehow, I still grappled with hope, too.

Lord, please let him like me. It's not my fault that I ended up in this mess. It's obvious I'm the consequence of stupid adults' actions. I wasn't really meant to be anybody's child.

I unclenched my hands and wiped the sweat on my shorts, hearing footsteps at the door.

Krisany sat on the edge of her seat and leaned toward me, wiping perspiration from her forehead.

What's wrong with you, Krissy? He's not your father.

Jack walked in and his head darted from Krisany to me. He shrugged and sat down in the chair.

"What's this, love?" Krisany reached across the table and flicked at the edge of a bandage beneath Jack's T-shirt sleeve. "I thought you stopped."

Jack brushed her fingers away from him. "Things have changed, so it's back on."

I didn't know what the bandage meant but Krisany rolled her eyes and seemed to drop that topic of conversation.

"How are your daughters?" he said, filling the awkward silence.

"They're fine. How are you doing?"

"Fine." He cleared his throat and glanced up at me. "Who's this you've brought with you?"

I couldn't hold his gaze, dropping my eyes to the floor.

"Jack, this is Alice." Krisany shoved paperwork toward him and stood up. "This will explain everything."

Jack folded his arms across his chest. He leaned forward and took the paperwork, glaring at it with widened eyes.

"What?" He shoved back from the table and stood up, his chair tumbling into its side. "I have a kid?" He kept his eyes on Krisany but paced back and forth. "I have a daughter, are you bloody kidding me? She lied to me."

I unconsciously reached for Krisany but pulled my hand back. All of my fears were coming true. I stuffed my hands in the front pockets of my shorts.

Jack stomped closer to Krisany. "Did you know about this?"

"Beatrice said something when Alice was a baby," she said, keeping herself between me and Jack, "but she never told me the results of the paternity test and—"

"What? How many times have you written to me over the

years? You've never once mentioned that there was a possibility I may have a child." Jack threw his hands in the air. "I can't handle this."

Krisany moved toward the door to block his retreat. I stayed rooted where I stood, digging my fingers into my legs. My thoughts spun like a Ferris wheel.

I think I'm going to vomit.

Jack opened and clenched his fists, but didn't try forcing Krisany aside. Finally, he backed away, running his hands through his hair. "Okay, okay, tell me what happened."

"Jack, all of those things I told you in our letters about Beatrice, Alice has been witnessing it—and much worse. Lately, I've been letting her live with me and my daughters," Krisany said.

Jack grabbed a water bottle from the table and backed into the wall farthest from me. White-knuckled, he sipped, the bottle crushing in his grip.

I crossed my arms over my abdomen, dropped my chin, and squeezed my eyes shut. Did he also see the situation as my fault, just like Beatrice did. When I opened my eyes, Jack stood in front of me. The dented water bottle still in his hands.

"It's a miracle you've been living with Beatrice and are not addicted to drugs."

I leaned my head back against the wall, still not sure how much I trusted this man. "Is...is there anything you want to know about me?"

He rubbed the back of his neck, his gaze almost glazed over. "I can't believe your mother kept this from me. If I had known you existed—" He shuddered, his pallor turning a ghostly white. "I'm going to be ill. Lord, this is terrifying." His eyes seemed to really focus on me for the first time—eyes that looked much like my own. "I'm sorry you've had to endure so much. They need to burn in hell for what they've done to you."

"I try to stay with Krissy as much as possible," I said, thrilled that he wasn't blaming me. "In a few months, I'll be eighteen. I'm getting away from Beatrice and Miguel and going to university."

"That's good. I..." He ran his hand through his hair, acting like he didn't know what else to say.

"Why don't we all sit down and try again." Krisany motioned for me to follow. When I sat down beside her, she held my hand and stroked it.

Jack walked over to the fallen chair, picked it up, and set it on the ground. Sitting down, his gaze focused on me again. "Do you have an idea what you want to study at university?"

"I want to become a swimming teacher. I'm on the swim team."

"She's the star of the swim team," Krisany said.

Her interjection made me smile.

"Brilliant!" he said, the corners of his mouth lifting too.

Though I had a thousand questions I wanted to ask, I didn't want to ruin the positive momentum in the room. I decided that staying on topic was the safest course. "Did you go to university?"

"I graduated from Oxford and worked as an engineer."

He's smart and yet stuck in here. What a terrible fate to have to endure.

"Are you dating anyone?"

My eyebrows arched at his question. We had just met. Shouldn't concerns about my dating life come much later? "Um, yes...I just started seeing someone, actually."

"What's his name? Is he nice? When did you meet?" Jack's eyes darted from me to Krisany.

I didn't like the intrusive questioning but I answered them anyway, hoping we could steer into more topics about him. "His name's Chris. I don't know much about him yet. He seems nice and he likes to text me, a lot. We met at college. He saw me at swim practice and our friends introduced us."

"You better be careful and take it slow. After all, you're practically a Latin princess."

He had no right to tell me how to do anything. He was the one sitting in jail. My jaw hardened and my hand dug into Krisany's hand. She grimaced but didn't stop me when I scooted back from the table.

Jack unscrewed the cap from another bottle of water and took a sip. He leaned back with the open bottle clenched between his hands. "Has Krissy told you why I ended up in prison? When I was at Oxford, I went to a pub and had a couple drinks with my flatmate, Andrew Carson. I scuffled with Andrew. He had a gun and it went off."

Did somebody die? Blood pooled in my clenched fingertips.

Krisany shook her head. "Jack, really?"

He ignored her warning. "The owner phoned for emergency services. We ran to my car, and in our hasty exit, left the gun behind. There was weed involved."

"Really? And you just told me not to do drugs." I shook my head, becoming even more disgusted with the man across from me.

"Alice, that's enough," Krisany said.

Jack lifted the bottle to his lips and took a long drink, his eyes focused just above my head. "We sped down the wrong side of the motorway and there was a car accident—"

"Why do you have bandages on your arms?" Why not ask, he was already telling me the horrid deed that landed him here.

Jack sneered and finished the story. "I was taken to a hospital. Once I recovered from my injuries I ended up here, where I have remained ever since."

I shoved my shaking hands under my thighs, trying to hide how much my anger at him affected me. "Jack, why didn't you run from Andrew?"

"Alice, I don't have an answer for you. I'm not right in the head," he said in a gruff voice

"Obviously." My mother sure could pick 'em. He wasn't any better than Miguel.

Jack glared at me. "You have no idea what it's been like for the last seventeen and a half years—"

"I have no idea?" I threw up my hands and glared right back. "I've been in hell and you put me there."

Krisany stood up, planting her hands on the table between the two of us. "Well, it seems that we have all lost our minds, haven't we?"

I'd heard enough, but Krisany put her arm around me when I stood so I couldn't run for the door.

"I think you'll be better off without me in your life." Sighing, Jack rose to his feet. "I haven't been in your life thus far, and there's nothing I could offer you."

"Fine by me." I had already come to the same conclusion. "You won't ever see me again."

"As lovely as this experience has been for all of us, I think it's time for us to go into our separate corners," Krisany said.

Jack walked to the door and pounded on it, yelling for Hatman. "Get me out of here."

I stayed close to Krisany, watching him leave.

"Wait." He stopped at the door. "Stay away from Andrew Carson."

I scowled at his useless warning. "I would never want to be friends with anyone you know anyway."

"Andrew Carson is a bad man. Stay away from him." He left without another word.

***

On the way home, I sipped a cola and read a few more pages of Jack's journal. Even with how our meeting had ended, my curiosity about the man had not been completely curbed. I read about his job, clubbing with friends, and his longing to find a girl to settle down with. His anger toward Beatrice matched my own.

I don't understand why Beatrice keeps coming around, she has a boyfriend in that filthy drug addict, Miguel. I don't like to be around him. He disrespects Beatrice in every possible way, but she doesn't see it. Tonight, Krissy came over for a chat, a drink, and a kiss. We ranted about Miguel. Krissy can't stand him either. God only knows what Beatrice sees in him. I can't believe I was stupid enough to fall for Beatrice. Krissy assured me it happens to the smartest of men, but it makes me ill thinking I was seduced by her. Beatrice was pretty on the outside, but absolute hell on the inside. I need another drink and Krissy's loving embrace.

The last line made me laugh.

"What's so funny?" Krisany asked.

"I think Jack had a crush on you, too. He was ranting about Beatrice."

Groaning, Krisany turned the wheel hard to the left. "Your mother is a nightmare, and that's putting it mildly. I don't know what would have happened with Jack and I. Perhaps I could have kept him out of trouble, but I found Daniel. Sometimes, I wish I would have ended up with Jack."

I wasn't sure how I felt about that revelation, so I ignored it altogether. "I'm going to read the rest of this when we get home. The car ride is making me ill." I rubbed my stomach. My head throbbed like a bass drum.

***

On the settee I finished reading Jack's journal. What he told me in the prison matched what he wrote in the journal, except that the car crash on the motorway resulted in the deaths of two people. Still reeling from the shock, I closed the book and rested it on my knee. "My miserable life is the result of too much alcohol and a one night stand." I cried at the stupidity and unfairness of it all, clutching the book to my chest.

CHAPTER 8

Chris sat in the crow's nest of the Brickley Stone College's swim area with D.J., Lisi, Luke, Serena, and Krisany, watching Alice and Kariann's swim competition. The humid space smelled of chlorine, the retractable roof letting in cloud-covered gray light from outside. Below, the pool with it's thick lanelines sparkled a sky-blue colour. Chris looked around the packed stands. Were Alice's parents here? Pulling out his mobile, he sent her a text message asking if her parents had come. No answer—a response he had been getting a lot from her the last few days. He knew she was busy preparing for this competition, but he couldn't shake the feeling her lack of communication might mean something more. Was she pulling away from him?

Is she avoiding me? I don't want to lose her. I won't bother her about it, but if this behavior continues, Alice is going to hear about it.

The teams walked out to thunderous cheers, in first place stood Brickley Stone in their red and blue checkered swimming suits. Edgington was not far behind in the rankings. Compared to Brickley, Edgington's uniforms were more fashionable in their solid black swimming suits with white straps and trim.

After the opening team relays, Alice was up in the first individual event. Chris watched her take her spot at the starting blocks at the pools edge. Every inch of her uniform's black and white swimsuit, white swim hat, and black goggles looked perfect. When the buzzer sounded, Alice dove into the pool. Her superb crawl technique sped her through her laps with ease, beating her opponents by more than three seconds. The Edgington team and crowd erupted into applause. Chris and his friends jumped up and down with excitement.

During the swim break in the middle of the meet, Chris and D.J. walked down to the team bench to congratulate the girls on their success.

Chris smiled down at Alice who was eating a banana. "Terrific job. You're an amazing swimmer."

She didn't jump up into his arms like he hoped she would, but she did return his smile though she still had a mouthful of banana.

"Did your parents come?"

Shaking her head, Alice swallowed and took a drink from her bottle of water. "No, of course not," she said with a mirthless laugh. She rose to her feet, acting as if she wanted to say more so Chris bent his ear near to her lips. "That's asking too much of them. Don't you understand, I don't matter to them."

"That doesn't make any sense." He folded his arms across his chest, digging his fingers into his skin.

"Don't let it upset you, Chris. I've learned not to expect anything from them. It makes life a lot easier," Alice said with a laugh.

"Well, I'm here for you." He gave her a quick embrace and a kiss on the cheek. She tensed beneath his grasp. He pulled back. "What's wrong?"

"Sorry, it's nothing. Thank you for caring."

"Sure thing." Now if only he could get her to let down the wall she had erected between them. "Good luck with the next relay."

She nodded and turned to Roxey, who was showing the other girls the new swimming app on her mobile.

As soon as Chris returned to his seat, Krisany nudged him.

"Are they here, Chris?" she said amid the chatter of the crowd.

Chris glared at the ceiling and shook his head. "No, they ditched the competition. How could they do that to her?"

"Beatrice is beyond complicated and her fiance, Miguel, isn't any better." Krisany shrugged her shoulders. "At least she knows we're here." Her eyes flashed on something beyond him, and she frowned. Chris turned to see what had upset her and saw Lisi and Luke locked in an embrace.

"You're right, Krisany," Chris said, trying to pull her focus back to him before she embarrassed her daughter. "She does have us, and we're going to make sure she always does."

Krisany nodded and sighed, turning her attention back to the pool where the relay race was about to begin.

Standing on a starting block, Alice lifted her gaze to where they sat and smiled.

A tall man and a short, blonde woman caused a gasp to ripple through the crowd. The man in light-blue swim trunks and flip-flops stumbled along the poolside deck with the woman in her white bikini and flip-flops.

"Wait!" the woman shouted. "Don't start the race! I must say something!"

Beside Chris, Krisany groaned. "Oh Beatrice, don't do this."

Beatrice? The woman making a scene was Alice's mother? Chris's eyes snapped back to the woman and man who were clearly intoxicated. Beyond, he noticed Alice's face had drained of colour though she still stood on the starting block.

She ripped her goggles off, staring wide-eyed and open mouthed at the couple running to the announcer. The inebriated woman pried the microphone out of the announcer's hands.

"We wanted to let everyone know that this girl..." Beatrice pointed to Alice's huddled form at the pool's edge, "...does not have a penny to her name, and shouldn't be allowed on the swim team. She's a terrible daughter, and she doesn't deserve any kindness from any of you."

The crowd muttered like bees in a hive. Alice left her place on the block and ran over to the couple.

Over the microphone, Alice's pleading tone could be heard. "You never come to any of my events, and now you show up at this one, drunk. Go home, now."

A boo grew from the crowd at the standoff happening below.

Chris's body shook, his blood boiling inside. He clenched his hands, his pupils focused on one thing—the man and woman tormenting his girlfriend.

Rising with the rest of the crowd, Chris stepped over D.J. to make his way past the others. Three sets of arms restrained and forced him back to his seat next to Krisany. From the pool deck, Alice's expression, now locked on him, seemed to harden and turn away.

Two police officers raced in and took Alice's parents out of the building to thunderous applause.

"Everyone, please," the announcer said to quiet everyone down. The man followed Alice over to her team bench. Surrounded by her team and her coach Miss Kai, Alice didn't look up again, keeping her focus on the discussion happening around her. Even after the announcer left to speak with the other team, she didn't look his way.

The announcer returned to his seat. "The competition will continue!" he said to thunderous cheers.

Once again, Alice took her place on the starting block. At the sound of the buzzer, Alice dove in the water. Each vigorous stroke propelled her ahead of her opponent. She arose out of the water to thunderous applause. She had given her teammate who followed her in the relay a huge lead to work with. Alice was embraced by Miss Kai, but the smile on her face couldn't cool Chris's anger.

I'm glad she could still swim well after all that, but I still want to kill her mother and step-father. What were they doing? They're mad!

Even Edgington beating Brickley Stone College for the first time ever couldn't lift his spirits.

***

Back at Edgington, Chris pulled Alice aside from the pizza awaiting them.

"Congratulations, Alice, you swam great. What's the deal with your parents?"

Her eyes drifted away from him, to the table where the girls happily ate the pizza. "How should I know. All they ever do is embarrass the hell out of me. And this time, they managed to do it in front of one of the largest audiences possible."

"Why did they do that?" He reached out to touch her shoulder.

She shrugged him off. "You're one to talk, Christopher. You did the same thing."

"What? I did not."

"Yes, you did. When they were yelling those awful things for everyone to hear, you stood up and tried to run off. Don't try to deny it, I saw you. It's obvious you never cared for me. You're just a player." She turned and walked away.

"Whoa, hold on a moment, Alice." Chris chased after her. "I didn't do that. I was trying too—"

"I don't want to hear it."

"Alice, listen to me." He grabbed her elbow.

She jerked away from him, the depths of her hazel eyes clouding over. "Don't ever touch me again. In fact, don't phone me, don't text me. I don't ever want to see you again, Chris, so just leave me alone." She stormed away to join the swim team at the table, her hissed words leaving him rooted to the spot.

What's her problem? That did not go the way I thought it would.

D.J. walked up holding a plate of pizza. "Hey, mate, what's going on? Alice looks furious."

"She broke up with me," he said, still trying to figure out how to deal with the emotional dagger she stabbed him with. "She thought I was running off when you stopped me from running down to kill her mother and step-father. She didn't let me explain anything and started raging. What am I supposed to do?"

"I'm sorry, Chris." D.J. put a hand on his shoulder, which only gained him another glaring glance from Alice. "I had no idea how vicious they were. I still can't believe it. What parent in their right mind would publicly humiliate their own kid? No doubt they were drunk."

"I agree, it's disgusting. She doesn't deserve that." Chris couldn't stop himself from looking her way again. She ignored him completely, conversing with Kariann.

"Yeah, maybe just give her some time to cool down. What her parents put her through today was pretty wild." D.J. clapped his back, the closest thing he'd ever get to a hug from him. "Just imagine what they do to her at home."

A chill ran down Chris's body at the words, an image of Alice's bruised back coming to mind.

CHAPTER 9

I stood in the kitchen looking out the window into a back garden full of weeds. There wasn't a speck of grass in sight. The garden seemed to plead for help, as it sat desolate and alone under a blue sky with sunshine streaming down. Like the little garden, I felt alone. My real father was in prison and a jerk—he wouldn't be saving me from this unbearable life either.

Today Beatrice and Miguel would officially marry each other, and I wanted no part of it. Alas, here I stood, in my white bridesmaid's dress, which looked more like a hideous wedding dress. The tight long-sleeves exploded into very poofy shoulders. The whole A-line bodice of the dress shimmered in rhinestones, and had an even more unfortunate bulky skirt covered in pleats. The heavy dress made me ill, something far too juvenile for me to wear, but again, wearing it stopped Beatrice's nagging me about not supporting her special day.

At least Krisany would be at the celebration, the others I would avoid. I wanted nothing to do with those who Beatrice called friends.

"Alice, get your ass in the car," Miguel said coming down the stairs.

Pleasant as ever.

I made my way outside without a word, though the dress hindered my ability to do anything quickly. By the time I got out the front door, Miguel was already in the driver seat, glaring at me. Squeezing my voluptuous dress into the back seat took even longer, and yet Beatrice still hadn't come out of the house.

Miguel's eyes glared at me through the rearview mirror. "Any funny business during this celebration and I'll kill you tomorrow. Do you understand me?"

I nodded, though I imagined myself gouging his eyeballs out.

"Answer me so I can hear you." He reached back, but, hindered by his seatbelt, only could touch the fabric of my dress.

"I understand."

Miguel nodded and pulled out a flask from his suit coat pocket. Uncorking it, he took a drink and turned around, keeping the flask in his hand.

Beatrice stepped out of the house in her cap-sleeve, pastel-blue, crystal-covered princess ball gown. Picking up the material of her skirt, she ran to the car, opened the door and struggled to climb inside. "Be careful with your gown. I can take it back and get my money refunded tomorrow. I never should have bought something like that for such an ungrateful, little brat." She smiled at Miguel who took another drink from his flask and put it back in his coat pocket. "Did you tell her no drama?"

"Yes, *Mother*, he did," I said, answering for him.

Beatrice sniffed from the front seat and adjusted the tiara on her head. "Why don't you go jump in a pool somewhere and drown yourself."

I laughed, gobsmacked. She was the one who demanded I be present for her farce of a wedding. If it were up to me, I wouldn't have gotten into the car.

Beatrice turned on the water works, looking like she was about to cry. Miguel took off the shoulder strap of the seatbelt and put it behind him. "What did you say to her, Alice?"

Seeing his rising anger, I didn't reply.

Miguel turned around and reached for me, but Beatrice threw out her hand and gazed at her lover. "Baby, stop. We don't have time for this, we need to get to the church. We can beat her later."

I dug my fingernails into the palms of my hands and imagined driving the tiara into Beatrice's head.

"All right, love." Miguel leaned over and kissed Beatrice on the lips.

"I don't taste any alcohol, love," Beatrice said, taking his hand.

"That's because it's water, babe. Don't get used to it. I plan on indulging myself tonight," he said with a smile.

When do you not indulge yourself, you maniac?

"Save me a drink?" Beatrice asked.

"Every time, beautiful girl." Miguel started the car and pulled away from the house.

At the next traffic light that turned red, they started snogging. I shut my eyes and threw my hand over my mouth to stifle a groan.

Once at the church, I stood by the car, watching Beatrice struggle out of the car beneath her massive gown.

Krisany arrived a few moments later. She gave Beatrice and Miguel a quick hello and congratulations before turning to me.

"Alice, what did they say today?" Krisany whispered.

"They threatened me with beatings after the wedding."

"Nobody's going to touch you while I'm here." Krisany hooked her arm in mine, walking beside me into the church.

With the church filled, the wedding began. I walked down the aisle feeling every eye on me. I longed to disappear. I had no idea who any of the people in the congregation were—minus Krisany. I reached the end of the aisle but wasn't sure where I was supposed to go next.

Do I go stand by Miguel, or maybe by the vicar?

To my left, I noticed Krisany sitting on the bench. I liked the idea of sitting beside her best, but before I could put my thoughts into motion, Miguel motioned me to him. He wrapped his arms around me in a false hug and whispered through clenched teeth. "Alice, if you mess this up, I will kill you. Understand?"

I nodded only to receive another punishment from him, his lips pressed to my cheek.

"Good, go sit down, baby."

My horribly large skirt hid my shaking knees as I took my place next to Krisany.

Beatrice came down the aisle to the music of a stringed quartet. She handed me her bouquet of pink, red, and white roses, her expression one of frowning disappointment until she turned to Miguel. Sobbing in raptured joy, she smiled at the love of her life.

The urge to vomit was overwhelming. The vicar's droning voice floated over my head, zoning my brain out.

Why should I be subject to anything that makes Beatrice and Miguel happy when my life is so miserable?

"...I now pronounce you man and wife."

My thoughts flew back and I found myself sitting on the hard, wooden bench. I stood up and half-heartedly clapped my hands along with the rest of the attendees.

Thank God, it's over!

Beatrice reached for her bouquet. I thrust it in her hand and watched her and Miguel walk out of the Church to the adjacent gardens for their reception.

I waited to exit with Krisany, slowly walking out of the empty church.

She laughed at the spectacle Beatrice and Miguel made. "I can't believe the clothes."

"Right?" The red dress she wore looked so much better. "I hate this dress, Krissy." I pointed and cringed at the frilly frock on my body.

We both broke into laughter.

"It is hideous. Well, the good thing is, the wedding is over. What do you say we go have some fun?" she said, looking toward the party with couples drinking, dancing, and jovial shouting.

"Sounds good. I think there are some ice lollies over there. I'm going to get one," I said.

Krissy nodded and I walked away. I hadn't gotten very far before the "blushing bride" called me over with her nasally voice.

"Alice, come over here and meet my friend."

I inwardly groaned but obeyed, coming face-to-face with my mother and a tall man about 6'4". His light-brown hair made his green eyes sparkle. He gave me a smile and I returned it.

"This is my friend Andrew—"

He cleared his throat and glared down at her. "Edward, remember?"

Beatrice nodded and a blush climbed up her neck and cheeks. "That's right, this is Edward. Be nice to him." She added with a glare of her own to me.

When had I ever not been nice, especially with someone whose expression showed nothing but kindness toward me? "Hello, pleased to meet you."

"Hello, Alice. It's a pleasure to finally meet you."

"Finally?" I blinked, showing my confusion to Beatrice but she smiled up at Edward.

"Yes," she said. "Edward knew me when I was at university."

University? I read enough about her antics during that time in Jack's journal to want to steer clear of anyone from that period. "Well, I'd best be off. Enjoy yourself, Edward." There, I acknowledged him. Now she couldn't complain that I wasn't nice. I walked away, but Beatrice came up behind me and put her hand on my shoulder.

"Alice," she whispered, "don't talk to anyone. This is my day, not yours." She spun away from me, walking with a flourish of smiles for everyone else.

I shrugged at her demand. I had no desire to talk to any of the guests. At the ice lolly table, Edward approached me again.

"Hey, Alice, do you mind if I stand with you?"

Beatrice had told me to be nice, but she'd also told me not to talk to anyone. In this situation what else could I do but pick one.

"Uh...sure." I smoothed over my initial hesitation by gesturing toward the table full of ice lollies. "I can't wait to get a hold of one of those."

"I bet. You look nice in the dress, although it seems a bit much. Don't you think?" He chuckled.

I reached for two lollies, a strawberry and orange, and made sure nobody stood too close by. "I hate this dress, to be honest," I whispered, stuffing the strawberry lolly in my mouth. The yummy, sweet flavour also had a hint of something else.

I don't care about this bloody wedding, Chris or Jack... I'm going to have fun for one night, and enjoy myself.

"How are you doing?" Edward asked.

I rolled the almost completely melted lolly in my mouth to the side. "I'm glad the wedding is over." I blinked, shocked I'd been so forthcoming with a stranger.

"I agree." He licked the yellow, mango lolly in his hand.

I squinted at the sudden fuzziness happening inside my head. "I know you know my mother, but what about Miguel?" I tossed the first empty stick and placed the orange lolly in my mouth.

Edward frowned and his face flushed red. "I know your step-father as well." He raised the dripping lolly again to his lips.

"You don't like him," I said, twirling the empty, red lolly stick in my fingers.

Edward nodded with a smile. "That's correct. You're very observant."

I tried to avoid Beatrice's friends as much as possible, but this Edward guy seemed like a nice fellow. I staggered over to grab my third ice lolly. I had a hard time maneuvering between the tables and the wedding guest I had just met.

"Can I put my hand on your shoulder? You seem a bit unsteady, love." Edward looked down at me with his ever-present green eyes.

"I'm fine." I giggled. "I don't know why I'm unsteady. I was fine an hour ago."

"You do know that these have alcohol in them, right?"

"Oh, I didn't know, but it's making the wedding more fun." I placed my arm around his waist and we tripped along to an empty table.

"Let me get that for you, darling." He pulled out a chair and helped me into it. He also sat, taking the seat to my left.

"I've got it all figured out, while Beatrice and Miguel are on their honeymoon, I'm going to drive. I have a driving license. Do you want to see it?" I slurred.

"No, no, I'm fine," he said twirling his empty lolly stick in his fingers.

I sniffed, tears blurring my vision. "I can't even be with my boyfriend—he doesn't love me."

"Oh, darling, it's all right. I'm sure you'll patch things up. You're a beautiful girl," Edward said.

Through my tears, I saw his sparkling, green eyes and broad smile. He really did seem like such a nice man.

"Alice, are you okay?" Krisany said, rushing up to place a hand on my right shoulder.

"I'm just fine. Have you met my friend?" I sniffed and turned my head in Edward's direction.

"You're not okay." Krisany looked down at me—a frown on her red lips. "Wait here, I'll be right back." She brushed my shoulder and turned to rush away.

"Wait for what? I can't handle this." I stood, the hot tears streaming from my eyes blurred my vision.

Edward stood up too. I buried my face into his suit coat. Caressed by his lovely cologne, I clung to his suit coat as if we were ziplining over a canyon and he was my only protection above the dark abyss.

"Awe, don't worry, sweetheart. You'll be alright." He wrapped his arms around me.

"Really?" I sniffed and lifted my head.

"Of course you will." He patted my shoulder.

"I want to go home now." I sniffed, wiping running makeup across my face.

"That's a very good idea," Edward said, gazing at me with that kind smile of his. "Why don't I take you home?"

"Do you know where I live?"

"Yes, I know where you live." Edward pulled me along toward the car park. Everytime I tripped and he held me up, even in my poofy dress.

"In you go," he said, pushing me into the passenger seat of a vehicle.

"Wait! I forgot to tell Krissany goodbye." I tried to climb back out, but his pressure on my shoulder kept me seated.

"Not to worry. She'll understand." He tucked the massive folds of my dress in with me and shut the door.

He climbed into the driver's seat and clicked his seatbelt into place. "Now it's your turn, darling."

"Huh?" Maybe if my head wasn't so fuzzy, but I had no idea what he wanted.

Sighing, he reached into my personal space. My hands snapped up of their own accord to block his advance. He raised his eyebrows, easily out maneuvering my sluggish movements to grab my seatbelt and pull it across me. "There. Now I can take you home."

"Are you sure you know where I live?" Of all the terrible people my mother and step-father brought home, I'd never seen him before.

"Yes, I promise."

"Okay, but you can't come into my house. I'm all by myself and my parents are on their honeymoon." I sniffed, another bout of tears threatening to come.

"That's okay, I don't need to come in with you. We're just going to get you safely home."

My mind wandered with the fuzzy moving buildings outside. My vision refused to clear so I couldn't tell if I was really going home or not. I swiped at the window, but my hand missed and landed in the heap of fabric engulfing me. "This stupid dress is so ugly, but if I hurt it Beatrice will never forgive me." I started to cry again. "I'm sorry. I've had a really rough night with my mum getting married. My real dad doesn't like me, and my boyfriend broke up with me yesterday." I wiped the tears down my face. "It was such a sad wedding, I had an ice lolly. Just one...just one."

Edward appeared at the open car door beside me, pulling me from the seat. "Don't worry, sweetheart. Everything is going to be fine."

The whole ride had been a blur, but I managed to get up the stairs and slide the key in my door without my new friend coming with me.

CHAPTER 10

In the middle of practicing football drills in D.J.'s back garden, Chris found himself fending off questions about Alice.

"How are things with your girlfriend?"

Sighing, Chris grabbed the ball from D.J., wishing he'd stop with the juvenile grin. It wasn't helping him feel any better about the situation. "It's up and down, mate. We fight about texting, but more importantly, we haven't made up."

"Damn, Chris. How many times do I have to tell you? Chill out about the texts. You're probably making Alice crazy, and I told you she's nothing like Aaliyah." D.J. took the football from him. "And, if you don't mind, I'm going to score a goal right now while you think about what I just said." He ran toward the imaginary goal.

"Hey! You can't do that!" Chris took off after him.

"It's easy when you're acting like an idiot," D.J. said, his tone full of laughter. "Goal! Beat that mate." He kicked the ball toward the other side of the garden.

"Oh, I will." Chris ran at full speed after the ball, doing a fancy switch kick to send the ball into the opposite goal. "Oh yeah! That was beautiful!"

D.J. whistled. "Nice." He ran over to where Chris stood. Though panting, his eyes still sparkled. "Tell me, have you and Alice kissed?"

"Yes, we have." Chris wasn't even sure why he answered. It's not like he needed to defend himself. He knew he wasn't a complete failure at the whole dating thing.

"Have you bedded up?" D.J. wiped the sweat from his dark-brown hair.

"No." He sighed. They weren't even close to reaching that kind of a relationship. Maybe he wasn't any good at this afterall. "I'm lucky if I can get my arms around her and hold her for more than thirty seconds without her freaking out about something. Look at these weird text messages I received from her last night." Chris pulled out his mobile.

D.J. took the mobile and scrolled through the messages. "Stupid dress…I hate them…Ice lollies…stop this…" Blinking, D.J. looked up. "I don't think she's okay. Where was she?"

"She was at her mum's wedding. I don't know why they're getting married now after they've lived together for seventeen-years. It's weird, mate." Chris glanced at the flashing screen of his mobile.

"They've been bedding up this whole time and now they're getting married? No wonder Alice doesn't want to live with those people. I thought she lived with Lisi."

Chris nodded. "Remember the scene they made at the swim competition? They're not right in the head. They're mental, they are."

"Maybe that's her problem. Maybe she's mental." D.J. chuckled, a broad smile lifting his face.

Chris didn't like anyone speaking bad about Alice, even if they were broken up at the moment. He snatched his mobile back. "She's not mental."

"Well, what then?"

Chris scrolled through the messages again. "She sounds drunk."

"Have you seen her drunk before?"

"No."

"Mate, I'd be careful," D.J. said. "The last thing you want to do is go after her without knowing what's going on.

* * *

Chris walked into the house through the kitchen, stopping to pick up a chocolate biscuit, then went down the cellar stairs to his bedroom. Laying on his bed, Chris finally found the courage to reply to Alice's string of text messages. "It sounds like you had quite a bit to drink last night. I'm glad you made it home okay." He weighed the words before hitting "send". He wasn't looking to start a fight.

Within seconds, she responded. "There was this guy. I can't remember what his name was. He took me home, but I didn't let him in."

"He went back with you?" He'd heard plenty of stories about sleazy men spiking a woman's drink. Chris typed, clutching the mobile in a white-knuckled grip. "Drink as much water as you can before you fall asleep."

"Well, it's a little too late for that."

Oh no. He forced himself to stay calm. "That depends. How drunk were you last night?" He hit "send" and took a bite of the biscuit.

"I had these ice lollies."

"How many?"

"I don't remember six, maybe eight. I don't know."

Eight? Holy smokes! His ability to remain calm slipped even further toward the edge of no return. "Good Lord, how did you get home? Did you drive?" He hit "send", snatching another bite of the biscuit.

"No, Beatrice and Miguel made me ride with them. The guy, whose name I don't remember, brought me home."

Alice, what are you doing? "Did you get hurt?"

"I don't think so. I'm home, not in hospital, so probably not."

Lord, this is bad. Keep her safe. "Are you alone?"

"I think so."

"This guy, are you sure he didn't stay with you?"

"Hell no, I wasn't that drunk."

Chris shook his head and frowned at the lit screen, but couldn't stop himself from asking. "Who is this guy?"

"Someone I met at the wedding. I don't know who he is. I don't even know his name."

Chris sighed and drummed his fingers, letting the screen go dark. Maybe it would be best to physically check on her. He wrote the request using the most innocent excuse he could think of. "I'm sorry it was such a rough night. Do you want to meet me at the cinema?"

"What I really want is to get some sleep. My head is killing me."

Chris stuffed the last of the biscuit into his mouth. Maybe this was the time to be direct. "Okay, I just want to make sure you're all right. I want to see you."

"I've got a lot of chores, and after our fight at Edgington after the swim competition, I'm going to have to think about it."

CHAPTER 11

I buried myself in the blankets. The house, quiet and safe, helped me fall into a deep slumber. I awoke to noises coming from the kitchen.

Who is that? I thought I was home alone.

I went into the bathroom and collected the sleeping pills Beatrice and Miguel used. I also took the metal dustbin, grasping both handles to use it like a shield in front of me.

Walking down the stairs, I heard Beatrice's nasal laugh drift up to me.

I probably won't have to hit someone, but I'll keep the pills handy. It never hurts to be prepared. Beatrice turned when I entered the kitchen.

"What are you doing with the dustbin?"

I lowered it from my chest, trying to look like it actually held rubbish inside. "I was just taking it out."

"Fine, take it out, and answer the door. Tell whoever it is to go away. I'm on my honeymoon." Beatrice gulped down the last of her tea and sauntered up the stairs.

With the dustbin in hand, I answered the door. Standing on the threshold was a distinctively good-looking man.

"Alice, I wanted to check on you and make sure you were all right."

"Me? Who are you?" I asked clutching the dustbin until my palms hurt.

"We met at the wedding last night. I helped you get home. I

wanted to make sure you were jolly good," the man said with a slight smile.

"At the wedding last night, we met?" His green eyes were captivating, but I had no idea who he was.

"Yes, it was a bit of a rough night, but I got you home. Don't you remember?"

I shook my head and gave him a dull look.

"My name's Edward," he said, folding his hands together.

"What did you say your surname is?" I asked, sweat trickling down my arms.

"It's Dwight. Sir Edward Dwight. Isn't every good, old man knighted? Can I take that for you?"

I clutched the dustbin against my chest. "Oh, no. Thanks, I'm fine."

"How are you feeling this morning? Does your head hurt? I've got this remedy—a pinch of ginger, a sprig of peppermint, some pineapple juice and lots of gin."

I couldn't stop myself from chuckling at the last part.

Edward smiled down at me. "It's the gin, not the pineapple juice, or herbs and spices."

"No, I've had enough." I stepped onto the front porch and closed the door behind me.

His gaze never left my face, but he had the courtesy to back up and let me pass. "You had a bad night—your mum, your dad, your boyfriend?"

"What?" My mouth dropped open. How much of my personal life had I shared with this stranger?

"You told me you broke up with your boyfriend, and weren't happy with the marriage of your mother." He descended the front steps behind me.

I groaned. "My mother wouldn't be happy with that little nugget if it ever got back to her." When had I become such a blabbermouth?

"Don't worry, Alice. I won't tell anyone. It's just between us."

I turned at his chuckle. He stood just above me on the last step of the porch.

"I have known your mother and step-father for a long time, and…I don't like them." Nothing in his expression made me doubt that statement. It buoyed my courage. Had I finally found an ally that truly understood my situation?

Stepping down, I let the dustbin swing at my side. "You're not alone, I can't stand them, but I don't recall saying any of it."

We walked around the side of the house to the wheelie bin.

"Well…you were pretty drunk. What's this business with your dad not liking you?"

I leaned against the wheelie bin to look into his face. "It depends on if you're talking about Miguel or Jack."

"Who? What?" Edward's hands flew up to his chest.

"Never mind." I turned around and dumped the contents from the metal dustbin into the wheelie bin.

"Would you like to take a walk?" He asked, folding his hands together.

This Edward fellow doesn't like Beatrice, that's something we have in common. A walk? Why not? Anything to get me out of the house.

"Sure," I said. The dustbin landed with a clang in front of the wheelie bin, and we walked, side-by-side, down the street.

"You mentioned someone named Jack. Jack who?" he asked.

I didn't love the question, but I had brought up my father so I couldn't blame him for being curious. "He has been in prison for seventeen years."

"How did that happen?"

"I don't know." I folded my arms across my chest, wishing he would find something else to talk about. "I guess he was involved in a crime and killed people."

"Wow, besides being stuck with a mother like yours, your father is a convict. You really need to leave here."

Stopping, I looked up into his green eyes. "That's nothing compared to Miguel."

"What's wrong with Miguel?"

"Miguel's very manipulative, controlling, and...demanding." I whispered the last part—my gaze falling to the ground.

"I'm sorry. You shouldn't have to be dealing with a man like that." One corner of his mouth rose. "You know, I could get you away from all of it—a place where you'd be safe."

Yeah right. After surviving this long on my own, I had a hard time believing anyone could really help me. I rubbed my eyes but no tears came.

"What you need is your own flat—somewhere you can go where the adults in your life can't control or manipulate you," he said.

"I'm too young to get a place like that."

"I can help you." He smiled so broadly his teeth gleamed down at me.

My stomach flipped at so much perfection. I dropped my eyes to the pavement. "Yeah, thanks, but I don't need your help."

"I have a flat I don't use. I don't even go there. You'd be on your own." His smile broadened again. "Free to do whatever you want."

"Why would you do that?" It made no sense. I wasn't much more than a stranger to him.

Edward threw his hands in the air. "After everything I've heard about the situation you're living in, why wouldn't I?"

Miguel stepped on the porch and screamed. "Alice, get back in here. The *cellar* needs cleaning." The sneer he made before stomping back into the house made his intention clear—he wanted sex. I gritted my teeth and rubbed my stomach. Why couldn't he sleep when Beatrice did? That alone would make my life so much better.

Edward looked down at me with his penetrating, green eyes. "It's available anytime you want."

"I'll need to pack. Can I meet you at your car?"

He nodded and pulled a mobile out of his pocket. "Be careful."

Chapter 12

Chris sat sprawled in the passenger's seat of the van while Tara fiddled with the radio. She swiped a used lollipop from off her forearm and kept maneuvering through the winding streets of the neighbourhood toward Chris's job.

At a traffic light, Chris glanced to his right. He saw Tara smiling at the five chattering children in the back of the car. Returning to his mobile, Chris furiously typed in another message to Alice.

"Chris, are you texting that girl again?"

He sighed. "Yes. She hasn't responded to my text this morning, so I don't know if she can come with us to the cinema this weekend."

Chris's mobile chimed. Looking down, he sighed again, then muttered under his breath, "I'm texting you constantly because you don't answer, Alice. It's irritating to me, too." His hand tightened around the mobile at a second chime. She hardly ever responded twice in a row. But her words made his other hand clench into a fist. He rested it on his chin. "What does that mean?" He glared over at Tara, but she only raised her eyebrows.

Oh, I have a lot to tell you, Alice, so listen up. Forgive me if I'm interested in what you're doing during the day. He hit "send" with a roll of his eyes. *It's not like you tell me.* Reaching for his bottle of water, he held it in a white-knuckled grip and watched the screen flash again.

"Of course. Why wouldn't you go off with another guy when

you're so clearly dedicated to this relationship." He laughed, shaking his head.

Her next response made him clench his teeth. "I'm crazy?"

Behind him, Kenneth started kicking his seat. He whipped around to glare at him. "Kenneth, stop that."

His words might as well have been a machete for as fast as Kenneth's eyes watered up.

"Kenneth." Tara placed her hand on the little boy's shaking leg and rubbed his knee until the tears were sniffed away. "Stop kicking the chair, darling. Chris, what's going on, love?"

Tara offered him a soft smile of encouragement, but he was too old to fall for such motherly manipulation. He returned his gaze to the mobile instead. *Oh yeah? If you liked me so much then you wouldn't take so long to answer my texts.* He hit "send" and drummed his fingers on the mobile.

"You're working? I'm working too." Chris muttered to himself. "You need a break? A break from your mobile? Just hang up then. What in the—"

Another message arrived on his screen. "What utter nonsense." *Send a search party? A private detective? Untrustworthy is putting it mildly.*

He locked the mobile and rested it on his leg, unable to do anything with the seething emotions inside him but lean his head back. His effort to calm down failed and he picked the mobile up again and typed furiously.

Really? You're going to use that attitude with me? What a load of tosh. You're acting like a brat.

"Break up with you...be like everyone else in your life who leaves when things get hard. What are you talking about?" Wasn't he always the one reaching out? If anyone kept pushing to break up, it was her. He clenched his eyes shut, but his mobile chimed again.

"You don't care if we're together."

Groaning, Chris covered his face. He'd had about all he could take of all these unfounded accusations she kept hurling at him. "Good Lord, she's infuriating!"

"Let me guess," Tara said beside him, "all that muttering was her responding to you right?"

Chris sighed and rubbed his temples. When he lifted his gaze to Tara, he drilled her with a gaze as intense as her own. "Yes. She's mad, that girl is. She thinks my text messages are demanding too much from her." Picking up the bottle of water in the cupholder beside him, he drained the remainder of the water, basking in the cool liquid sliding down the back of his throat.

Tara smiled. "Darling, listen to me. You've got to stop texting her so much. You're going to push her away. Didn't you tell me she has been less responsive to you lately?"

"Yes, but…" Something about the situation seemed so wrong, he felt compelled to keep trying to reach her.

"Chris, you need to take it easy." Tara put her hand on his shoulder. "You're acting a bit, well…a bit obsessive, and I think you're scaring Alice away."

"I am not being obsessive." He frowned and shook his head, unable to shake the constant worry Alice brought to his mind. "I think she's got some other stuff going on that she's not telling me about."

Tara's deep frown wrinkled her forehead. She glanced at him. "Why are you worried about her?"

"All I know is her parents yell a lot. She never elaborates, but I've heard them when they ring her up. Her step-father sounds very intimidating. I don't want to lose her like I lost my mum. I couldn't handle that." Chris tried to peel Tara's ever-present gaze from his view as he stared out the windscreen, fidgeting with the darkened mobile.

"I see. Is it possible Alice thinks you're coming across a bit intimidating, like her step-father. I mean, the way you want to talk with her all the time... Does she know your intensions? Have you told her about your fear of losing her?"

"I can't tell her about my mum, Tara?" Chris's gaze flickered to his step-mum. "I want to make sure she's safe, not to scare her."

"You know, opening up to her could help her understand," Tara said.

"Maybe..." Or such a confession could be the worst thing he ever shared. Right now, he was too scared to find out for sure. "But now is not the right time. She's very shy."

"Christopher." Tara's eyes narrowed and she pursed her lips. "I'd tell her sooner rather than later. Opening up your own heart will help your relationship."

Chris laughed, hoping a good dose of bravado would hide his lack of courage. "That's not happening, Tara."

Tara sighed but focused on the windscreen again. "I'm just saying, son... From my own experience, if a boy was texting me constantly, I'd shy away from him."

"Uh huh." Chris sighed and nodded, turning to watch his younger siblings banter back and forth about sports or dance being more fun.

"It makes you wish Alice's worries were as little as your sisters and brothers, doesn't it?" Tara asked with a broad smile.

Chris couldn't disagree with the constant low-level chaos happening in the back. "Yeah, they drive me insane most of the time, but they do make it easier to forget my own problems."

***

Biscuits and Confetti Bakery sat nestled in a row of shops in the center of town. Chris leaned against the car, rolling his eyes at the Biscuits and Confetti sign in deep-golden lettering with bright-coloured confetti surrounding the words—a sign that encapsulated the craziness of his job—but he loved it.

Chris herded Tara and his five younger siblings through the glass doors. Biscuits and Confetti smelled of fresh baked bread, chocolate, and butter. The white, tile floor, with big, colourful, confetti-patterned-splotches, sparkled in the streaming lights overhead. Brightly coloured pictures of baked goods and dishes lined the sunshine-yellow walls.

Tara directed the five children to sit at one of the plastic tables in the front of the shop. Chris slipped back to the white cabinets to dress in his apron and baker's hat. After wiping down the stainless-steel worktop, he handed Tara some of the shop's free samples. He could have taken them all, his boss, the owner of the bakery, Giuliana Birkenshire, would not have minded. In fact she brushed back her ginger-coloured hair, then folded her plump fingers beneath her doughy chin, her sparkling, green eyes dancing over the children.

Once they finished their treat, Tara motioned the children to stand with her at the front of the queue.

"Awe, Tara, how are you and the children today?" She propped her elbows on the worktop and smiled at the five little ones.

"Giuli, you might want to cut down on the chatting," Chris said, walking past the counter. "You've got more customers."

The queue behind Tara had grown so long, she quickly ordered bread, croissants, and a few jars of Buttered Bliss before nudging the children aside.

Chris did his best to keep the orders flowing, with his boss's love of gab it was a challenge. He also had to contend with his younger siblings. Kanene winked every time he looked her way. Emmalyn followed him around, asking him every question that popped in her head. Chris did his best to answer her many questions.

"Do you think I could work here when I'm older?" Emmalyn looked up at him with a sweet, innocent expression.

"That's not up to me, Emme." Though he thought Giuli should probably think twice before hiring her. With how much his sister talked, Giuli might never get any work done again if Emmalyn worked here.

Standing behind the service counter, Chris watched Tara struggle to gather the children to leave.

"Well, have a great day, Chris." Tara flashed a smile but he knew better, the kids were wearing on her patience.

He walked over to the table where his younger siblings fought over their mother's mobile. "Boys, give me that." He snatched the mobile out of Gavin's hands and glared a "frigid blast" at each boy.

"Chris, let me handle them. You go on," Tara said, walking over. She took her mobile from his hands like she had everything under control, but was it just an act.

"Chris?" Tara put a hand on his shoulder. "Are you all right?"

Sighing deeply, he looked at her intensely. Did women ever really say what they mean, or were they all like his mother, hiding behind false words and smiles? "Tara, if I ask you something, will you tell me the truth? Even if it's about my mum?"

Her eyes narrowed, and her mouth gave a slight frown, but her gaze never left his own. "Yes, but I think it best if we have this conversation later—away from the children."

Chris nodded. "Thanks, Tara. I'll see you later."

She gave him a gentle push toward the service counter. "You'd best be getting to work, sweetheart. See you tonight."

Back in the kitchen, Chris started to make Giuliana's award-winning Buttered Bliss.

8 ounces butter, whipped in a mixer,
4 ounces honey
2 ounces maple syrup
½ teaspoon freshly-grated nutmeg

The mixture became a deep golden colour, rich in flavour, when heated. Tasting like butter and fresh honey from the honeybees, Buttered Bliss's silky smoothness made any food you filled or spread it on taste spectacular!

With the Buttered Bliss made, Chris made Giuliana's equally famous pound cake.

Whipping the honey and butter into a frothy blend in a large pot, Chris added the nutmeg and maple syrup. He sunk his teeth into his lower lip, his thoughts creeping back through the fight he had with Alice via text message on the drive over.

Slabs of rich butter melted and ran down the sides of the pot, forming a yellow pool on the honey mixture's surface. Chris's tensions from the earlier texts slid with the melting ingredients into a larger puddle of anger and ache.

The mixture heated, sizzled, and bubbled up from the recesses of the pot. Chris tightened his jaw, a slight nausea rising in the back of his throat. Swallowing the bile, Chris clutched the massive wooden spoon, plunged it deeper into the honey and butter, and circled it in wider patterns throughout the mixture.

With his teeth clenched and mind absorbed with life beyond Biscuits and Confetti, Chris's vision closed around the flashing letters of Alice's many harsh texts.

The liquid turned a light golden colour, foaming and hissing as it moved around. Clouds of steam rose from the pot. Chris scraped the sides, the liquid continuing to bubble around the wooden spoon in his white-knuckled grip. Liquid lava inside the boiling pot splashed on his hand.

Gasping, he dropped the wooden spoon inside the pot. "Bloody hell, it's burning. My skin is burning…" He ran to the sink, soaking the blistering skin in cold water. "All thanks to you, my dear." He never should have let the situation with Alice distract him from his job, but getting her out of his head seemed impossible. He glared at the burn on his hand. "Everything between us is stupid, and I'm tired of it." He pressed a cold tea towel to the burn and turned away from the sink only to catch Giuliana running toward him.

Gaping, she clutched her pudgy fingers in front of him. "Chris, what happened!" She eased his hand from the tea towel to inspect it. "Ooo...that looks bad," she said, her eyes pooling with unshed tears.

"Yeah, it bloody hurts." He gestured to the pot on the stove. It needed to be taken care of before they lost an entire batch to a scorched bottom.

Giuliana nodded. "But let me help you first." She rushed to a cupboard in the corner of the kitchen. Opening it, she picked up a white bowl with confetti dotting the surface. She filled it with ice and cold water and brought it back to Chris.

He immersed his hand in the icy liquid.

"How does that feel?" Giuliana rushed to the stove and turned down the heat.

"Better." Chris sauntered over behind her, keeping his hand submerged. "Thanks Giuli. Note to self, don't fight with someone then stir foaming, hot liquid." He laughed.

Shaking her head, Giuliana used a different spoon to fish out the wooden one he'd dropped inside the pot. The whip of her stroke showed her years of experience making Buttered Bliss. "Chris, I don't mean to get in your business, but I couldn't help see you coming in here furious." She looked over, searching his face. "What's going on? Did you and your girlfriend get into a row again?"

He wasn't even sure if she *was* still his girlfriend. Chris shrugged his shoulders and sighed. "Yes, it feels like whenever she finally feels like texting back, it's only to fight." He lifted his hand out of the bowl and gently fingered the border of the burn. "Lord, it hurts." He winced and resumerged it. "She says it's because she needs space, but I think I'm being reasonable."

Giuliana nodded and fingered her apron in thought. "Chris, it's fine to care about someone and want to be with them every minute of the day, but I think you should try to let her have some freedom. Has she ever cheated on you?"

"No..." Chris bit his lip and bowed his head, shifting his weight from foot to foot. "But I still worry she might."

"Why is that?"

"Well, Aaliyah, my biological mum, left my dad for another man when Kanene was just a baby, and—" He stopped, the pain of having his heart opened stitch by stitch almost more than he could bear. The tears he wished he could hide rolled down his cheeks. He cleared his throat, trying to compose himself.

"I see... So it sounds like you're thinking your girlfriend will do the same as your uh..."

"Aaliyah—her name is Aaliyah. She has no part in my life, and I want to keep it that way." Chris lifted his burnt hand again. He clenched it into a fist, giving into his temper until a sharp pain reminded him of why he shouldn't. Grunting, he dropped his hand back into the water. "That bloody hurts."

"Sounds to me like you're pressing this girl into the same mold as Aaliyah, and that's not fair. I really doubt your girlfriend would cheat on you, Chris. You are such a good, young man. I'm sure she sees that, too." Giuliana's green eyes sparkled, her entire face lifted with a smile.

Rolling his eyes, Chris laughed. "Yeah right. She was raging at me when we were texting earlier. Plus, I get the feeling she's got other problems going on that she's not telling me about. I know her parents are horrible to her, but she won't tell me anything else."

Giuliana adjusted her white baker's hat. "I see. That is an adventure the two of you will have to travel together. Give it time, Chris. She'll start to open up to you."

Walking to another cupboard, Giuliana pulled out a tube of burn cream and returned to Chris. She slathered half the tube on the surface of the burn until the blistering burn disappeared behind a cloud of ointment.

"That's going to hurt for a while, even after the heat is gone."

Giuliana's sparkling eyes drifted over Chris's face until he wiped his cheeks and stared at his trainers.

"The Buttered Bliss is to blame," she said. "It wasn't your girlfriend, or anyone else who made the mark, and the healing will come when you are ready to let the cream do its work, and you trust yourself enough to try again."

Chris's pulse thudded beneath the cloud of cream on the burn, his thoughts reflecting on the numerous scars on Giuliana's hands.

"Giuliana, you have so many scars." Chris slid his fingers along the scars on her right hand, as if he were touching the wings of a butterfly.

Giuliana covered his hand with her own. "Wounds leave scars, Chris—marks of our lessons and mistakes. That's how we learn not to reach into the Buttered Bliss ever again." She turned off the stove and poured the hot liquid into the awaiting jars.

Chris watched the steaming liquid flow from the pot like a golden river to rest in each jar.

"Every time I work with the Buttered Bliss, I learn more about how to work with it. I always assume it will burn me if I'm not careful. I have to give it the room it needs to become the best-selling item in the shop."

Giuliana moved the jars to be sealed up in the water bath. "Chris, you need to cut back on the texts, and give her some room to breathe. Have a bit of faith. Not every woman's going to be like Aaliyah. I promise, things will work out."

* * *

When Chris walked into the house, Tara herded the children into the back garden.

"I need you to play while Chris and I have a talk."

Once they were all good and distracted, Tara returned to the patio and sat on the bench next to Chris.

"All right, Chris. Your mum—what do you want to know?"

"Did she really leave us because of another man?" Chris bit his bottom lip to stop its quivering. Saying his greatest fear out loud made heat rise in his cheeks. He clenched his hands and looked away, but her lack of response stretched on for so long he gave up trying to hide his tears and turned to her.

She stared out with a pained expression, her hands wringing on her knee. Finally, she sighed and stole another glance toward the younger children. Opening her handbag, she pulled out a package of tissues and handed them to Chris. "You're old enough now to know the truth. Aaliyah didn't just run away from your dad, Kanene, and you to be with a man." She put an arm around his shoulders. "Chris, your mum reached a point when she just couldn't deal with raising you and Kanene—"

"So, it *was* my fault." Chris pushed her away and rose to his feet.

"Oh, Chris, that's not what I meant, sweetheart." Tara stood and placed a hand on his shoulder. Her voice took an even gentler tone. "When your dad went back to school to become a solicitor, trying to take care of you and Kanene became too much for her. She was used to your dad doing everything for her, but with his career change he couldn't—that sent her spiraling. She had some postnatal depression with Kanene, and began to loathe herself. She cried constantly and tried to cut herself. When your dad took measures to stop her from doing it anymore, she moved on to drinking, because she didn't know how to help herself get away from the chasm of despair inside her. But both you and your sister were her angels. She loved you more than anything in the world. The last thing she wanted was to hurt either one of you."

"Yeah, she really shows that now." He gave a mirthless laugh and swiped at the tears falling down his cheeks.

Tara sighed and pushed him to sit. After a moment of hesitation, he finally did.

"Chris, I can empathize with Aaliyah. I understand what it's like to raise children on your own, without a supportive husband."

She put a hand up to stop him from speaking. "I'm not saying what she did was right or how she handled things was correct, but as a mother, it's hard to be on your own every day with kids. While you were in primary school, your mum started going online. She reconnected with a secondary school boyfriend, and they ended up having several rendezvous and…"

"What happened? What did she do?"

The fingerpainting happening at the picnic table drew Chris's attention. It brought back the memory of finger-painting with his mother. He threaded his fingers together and bit his cheeks, but even that didn't stop another flood of hot tears from coming.

"She invited her lover to come around when dad was gone," Tara said.

Chris's eyes widened, and his mouth fell open. "You're kidding... Wait! It was the man who came around all the time, wasn't it? Aaliyah said he was helping repair the house, but he wasn't doing anything of the sort. Poor Kanene, she was in the house when this was going on. What if something had happened to her?"

"No, no, she's fine, love. But when your father came home and found the two of you alone, he packed up your stuff and took you two away." Tara folded her hands together and looked down at her wedding ring, a broken smile on her lips.

Chris sniffed several times as he nodded. "I don't understand how she could do what she did." He rubbed his stomach. "I feel ill."

"Darling," Tara said, wrapping her arm around him, "none of this is your fault. Your mum—"

"Aaliyah," Chris interjected, shooting her with a scowl.

"Right," Tara said with a slight laugh. "Aaliyah made her choice—it was alcohol, a secondary school boyfriend, and another new baby—"

"No, no, stop. I don't want to know."

"She has a new family, but so do I. I love you, and I'm not

going anywhere…all right?" A wide smile lifted the corners of her mouth and her dark eyes sparkled.

Chris didn't feel like smiling back. He sighed and looked over her shoulder at the sunset.

"Are you all right?" She grabbed his chin and forced him to look at her.

"I guess. It's a lot to take in, but Dad should have never lied to me. I had no idea what was going on. It's so irritating."

Tara frowned and shook her head. "Christopher, your dad didn't mean to lie to you. He was trying to protect you from Aaliyah's horrible behavior. Telling you that she ran was him loving you. Aaliyah was the problem, your dad did everything he could to better your lives. Sometimes, I need to remind him to help me." She rolled her eyes. "But he's honest, he has integrity and drive, and that's the most important thing in a man. None of you deserved any of this. I love you, Chris." She pulled him into a tight embrace that he didn't struggle away from. "I want to see you begin to heal yourself, but that can only happen if you find a way to forgive Aaliyah. It's your choice, and whatever you decide to do I'll be here to support you."

"Thanks, mum. I love you too." The title fit her so well it brought a slight smile to his lips. He should have said it sooner.

Chapter 13

Pulling up to a house brought a pang of fear rolling around my stomach. I clenched the straps of my backpack and glanced at Edward. "This is your flat?"

"Oh, no. We'll go there later, but you need to meet someone else first. Why don't you come in with me?" He smiled, but I trusted his gesture of friendliness even less.

"I'll just wait for you." I folded my arms across my abdomen, my fingers digging into my skin.

"Are you sure? It's just for a moment."

"That's all right. Give me an address and I'll walk there myself. I don't want to go into the house." I shied away from his leaning body encroaching into my space until I realized he was pulling out his mobile.

He sent a text and sat back. I looked from him to the radio he turned up, unsure of what I should do next.

The house's front door opened and a tall slender woman walked out to the driver side window. Edward wound the window down and introduced us.

"Hello, love. Alice, this is my wife, Layla. Layla, this is Alice," he said, smiling at me.

"Hello, Alice. It's so nice to meet you! I've heard so much about you already." Layla's warm brown eyes held my gaze. She had lovely, dark-blonde, curly hair flowing down her back.

Nothing about her expression or appearance seemed threatening so I relaxed a little more. "Hello, pleased to meet you."

"I was going to take Alice to the flat. Why don't you come along with us?" Edward said.

"All right, I'll join you." Layla smiled.

I climbed out of the car and into the backseat.

On the way to the flat, Layla told me about her clothing store. "It's called the Coral Clover."

"Oh, yes, I know where that is. It's next to Biscuits and Confetti. I've been there many times." Though I didn't mind the small talk, I still clutched my backpack to my chest.

"Really? That's wonderful! Alice, do you play any sport? You look so athletic." Layla prattled off another question from the passenger's seat.

"Yeah, she's on Edgington College's swim team." Edward said before I could even answer.

"Excellent! Alice, you would be the perfect model for the Coral Clover. You have the perfect body—your skin and hair are gorgeous." She turned around and gave me a broad smile that showed off her gleaming white teeth.

Heat rushed to my cheeks from all the praise. I bowed my head, but she wasn't done making me the center of her focus.

"What else do you do?"

"Oh…I do quite a lot, but I'm focused on my studies and swimming right now." I played with the zipper on my backpack. I had no idea what to say to these kind strangers. The compliments they shared on my behalf made me extremely uncomfortable, and I didn't want to divulge anything more about myself. Luckily, Layla launched into an explanation of what clothes she would love to see me wear. Edward joined in with happy exclamations, allowing me to remain silent, for which I was most grateful.

At a block of flats, Edward led the way past a smiling doorman into a bright foyer. The white tile floor gleamed as we walked toward the lift bank, opposite the front door. A hint of apple cider and cinnamon floated in the air. I noticed a large seating area with a plethora of fine upholstered settees and armchairs sitting on plush tan carpet. A sparkling white fireplace with matching mantel sat at attention with a roaring fire inside. The warm foyer chased the chill away from the autumn afternoon air.

A concierge smiled at our approach. "Mr. and Mrs. Dwight, good to see you again."

The lift carried us to the fifth floor. Edward directed me to flat, 5A, directly across the corridor. Unlocking the door, he stepped back and allowed me to enter the large one-bedroom flat first.

The nautical themed decor used a lounge and large picture window as the focal point. Coral drapes adorned the window with an oversized teal fabric settee below. A large, multi-coloured rug covered the wooden floor. On the wall, opposite the settee, hung a clock and a flat screen television.

In the kitchen, a plush, white rug sat beneath the walnut table and two chairs. The worktops were made of black marble and had stainless appliances. It didn't matter that the room was small, I'd never lived in such elegance in all my life.

The bathroom, off to the right when you walked in, had the same sparkling, white floor as the foyer of the building. A black marble worktop accented the small vanity and white square sink. The same white tile as the floor lined the separate bath and shower. A toilet in the back finished off the room.

The bedroom sat at the back of the flat. As the largest room in the flat, it held a king-sized bed draped in a fluffy, sand-coloured quilt. A white blanket covered with fish, palm trees, and pineapples sat at the foot of the bed. Two ocean-blue pillows rested at the head of the bed, leaning against a light brown leather headboard. Two white bedside tables flanked the large, cozy-looking bed. Pictures capturing the beach during the day and at sunset lined the walls.

I did a slow circle, my mouth gaping open. There was heat and nobody lurking around to beat me up. I couldn't believe my luck.

"What do you think, Alice?" Layla put a hand on my shoulder. "Do you like it?"

What else could I do but nod? I had given up trying to keep my expression neutral not long after the tour started. I walked over to the settee bathed in sunlight from the picture window. Sitting down, I let my backpack slide to the floor. "I love it. Thank you."

"I'm glad," Edward said with a smile. "You're welcome to stay here until you go to university. I know you're not comfortable with men…" He walked to the settee and pulled a card out of his wallet, "…so here's Layla's mobile number. Layla can be your contact if you need anything. Here's the key to the flat and my number, in case anything needs to be repaired."

I looked from the cards and key in my hands to his face. "Edward, are you sure about this?" I wasn't used to such generosity coming from others.

He smiled even broader. "Of course I am. After all you've been through, I think you need a bit of independence to show your mother—" He grimaced, "— and others that you can manage life on your own, and they don't need to worry about you."

"All right." I rose on shaking legs, overwhelmed by this couple's kindness. "Thank you again, Edward."

"Oh, Alice. Before we go, could I take your picture?" Layla asked.

I furrowed my brow at her odd request.

"I mean just your face today. I really do think you'll make an excellent model for Coral Clover, and I would like to show my associates. If you don't mind?"

With such gushing compliments, how could I say no? I stepped to the wall Layla directed me to.

She took a picture with her mobile and beamed. "That is brilliant! Alice, you're a natural for this kind of job."

"Wait." I liked her enthusiasm but I didn't want to lie to her. "With my studies and swim team competitions, I don't know if I'll have time for a full time job."

"Don't worry about that, love. We'll work around college, homework, swimming, your friends, whatever you need. I just know you're going to love your experience at Coral Clover. You're going to look stunning on advertisements!"

"All right. That sounds great." I'd never had anyone believe so wholeheartedly in my abilities. For the first time, in a long time, I didn't have to force my face to smile.

* * *

I loved living by myself. Each night, I cleaned and ensured the front door was locked, but the rest was taken care of. I spent my day at Edgington and worked with Layla at the Coral Clover. Layla ensured nothing interfered with swim competitions or college. Edward even dropped off groceries.

One morning, as I rushed around getting ready to go to Edgington, Layla phoned me.

"Hello, Alice. Could you drop by the shop this afternoon? I've got some new clothes I want you to try on and model for the new round of advertisements."

"Sure, I can do that," I said, picking up my backpack.

"Wonderful. One more thing, a lady named Krisany rang the shop this morning, asking if you're okay. I assured her you're fine, but she seemed upset and mentioned telling your mother."

I've been gone over five weeks, and now they're wondering where I am?

"Don't worry about it. I'll let her know I'm all right. Thanks, Layla," I said, walking out the front door.

***

The Coral Clover was nestled among other shops in the center of town. The clothes were lovely, but I had never purchased anything. I needed every penny I had to keep my mobile on and pay for lunch. However, Lisi and most of our friends bought clothes from The Coral Clover. Thanks to Lisi's generosity, I was able to wear some of the clothes too.

The Coral Clover sign had a deep, ocean-blue background, with "The" painted in red, "Coral" in coral, and "Clover" in yellow. Seashells in light pink and glossy white, along with silver pearls, bordered the sign. The cheerful sign welcomed everyone that stepped through the glass door of the white, brick-clad building.

The soft scent of vanilla drifted to my nose when I stepped through the doorway onto the coral stone floor. A massive crystal chandelier hung in the center of the room over the cosmetic and accessory area. Soft, classical music played from speakers in the ceiling, while numerous ladies and girls browsed the shelves, tables, and racks of clothes.

Layla nodded and waved Edward over. Together they led me through the shop to the back. She waved and gave friendly hellos to the customers and employees we passed.

Once in the stockroom, Layla closed the door and walked over to the boxes in the middle of the room. My gaze went beyond, to the rows of boxed jeans, tops, dresses, swimwear, accessories, perfumes, cosmetics, candles, and undergarments stacked on the shelves lining the room. It seemed The Coral Clover had everything a girl could ever want when she stepped through the glass front door.

Layla handed me a pair of jeans and opened another box. She pulled out a deep, sea-blue tank top with rhinestones lining the neck and thin straps.

"Here, Alice, try these on." Layla turned to her husband. "Edward, get the camera ready. We're going to the changing rooms."

I followed Layla to the changing rooms without a word.

The outfit was a perfect fit. Layla shrieked in delight when I came out of the changing room. "Oh, Alice, that looks fantastic, darling. Here's some earrings, put them on. There we go... Edward, you're on." She stepped out of the way.

Between all the camera flashes, I tried on a few secondary school uniforms, not the most stylish, but they were what the secondary schools required. Followed by a couple of sun dresses in pink and white stripes, and a navy-blue, green, white and pink tie-dye.

The bathing suits were my favourite to model, bringing me back to the element I liked most—water. I showed off their first choice—a long two-piece with a black and white checked top. The white straps criss crossed in the back. It even came with a black skirt, which gave me even more confidence for the camera. Then came the bikinis, but with each new design I slipped on, I grew more comfortable with the ever-present stare of the camera and the onlookers. It wasn't long before I was back in my regular clothes.

Edward and Layla poured over the pictures I had done. They made comments about my work being perfect and both liked the swimwear photographs the best—particularly Edward. He kept looking at me with a big thumbs up with every bikini picture Layla pointed out.

Business hours flew by, and it wasn't long before Layla and I were locking up the shop.

Layla rummaged through her handbag for the keys. "Alice, I have a friend who's a clothing designer, and he's looking for a model. He's passing through England on his way to Italy. I told him about you. He would like to meet you. Is it all right if he stops by the flat tomorrow?"

"I suppose..." It would be rude to refuse. Layla had been so kind to me, and now she was trying to get me more work as a model. "Is there anything you want me to tell him?"

Layla shook her head and chuckled. "Oh, don't worry about that, sweetheart. I'll make sure he knows how wonderful you are."

Her smile brought a smile to my face. The kindness of this woman and her husband still amazed me.

"All right. It sounds exciting."

CHAPTER 14

Chris slouched against the settee, wrestling with the idea of texting Alice. A plate of chocolate biscuits sat on a table next to the settee. Steam rose from a cup of tea, mocking his discontent. He hadn't reached out to her via mobile for weeks now, but he couldn't shake the growing worry he had over her. They still had short interactions at Edgington, but even those seemed to be happening even less. Finally, he just gave in.

"Hey, Alice! The last time I met up with you at Edgington it was outside of chemistry, but we haven't been in touch since. What's up?"

"Hey, Chris."

Really? That's all she was going to say? Couldn't she at least answer the question? His mobile vibrated again. He let out a breath, grateful he hadn't started texting his frustration at her two-word response right away.

"Sorry, I've been so busy, but it has been quiet ever since my Mum and step-father got married."

Quiet? That didn't make any sense after the marks he had seen on her body. Chris ran his fingers through his hair. Maybe she wasn't being honest because someone was monitoring her.

"Are you okay?"

"Hunky-dory!"

Her bloody step-father bashed her up and now everything is 'hunky-dory and quiet'? Chris wiped a drop of tea from his bottom lip. Texting didn't offer a tone like talking did, so it was hard to know for sure. Maybe if she would meet him, but he wasn't quite brave enough to ask that just yet. "Where are you, love?" He frantically typed.

"I have a new job. I'm a model for The Coral Clover."

Before he could form an adult response to the twisted tangle of emotions rolling through him, another text appeared.

"I'm making money so I can save for university."

Chris shook his head. "I know we never patched things up, but when did this happen?"

"After the wedding. Beatrice's friend who drove me home gave me the job."

"Beatrice? Is she your mother?"

"Yeah."

"You trust Beatrice's friend?"

"Krissy's friend, too!"

Chris stared at the lit screen for what he could have sworn were hours before his mind released his fingers to reply. "Well, if you're alright, I guess I'll talk to you later." What else could he say and not end up in a fight? He truly hoped she was okay.

"Yes, I hope you're doing well. I've got to go to work now. Talk to you soon."

Did that mean she would finally contact him first? Probably not, but he would have to wait days before reaching out again or she might accuse him of coming on too strong. Sighing, Chris frowned at the lit screen. "Okay."

Chris's father walked in and sat down. "Son, can we talk?" He placed his mobile next to him on the armrest.

"Sure." Chris knew this would be coming after the talk with his step-mum. Tara didn't keep secrets from his father. He set his mobile down beside him, and gave his father his full attention.

"Tara told me that you two discussed Aaliyah. What do you think about all of it?"

"I think you should have told me the truth from the very beginning."

"I was trying to protect you, Chris."

Chris clenched his fists and glared at his father. "Why protect me from the truth? Did you think I couldn't handle it, so the best thing you could do was lie to me? Is that what you thought?"

Hugh folded his hands together on his knee. "Yes. I thought if I told you what happened, you'd have a harder time dealing with it."

Chris rose to his feet. "But the way you talk made it sound like you blamed me. That was unfair!"

"Christopher, listen to me," Hugh said, standing. He placed a hand on Chris's shoulder. "At the time, I was under a lot of stress, trying to raise two kids, a career change, and trying to make sure you didn't go without. I had to say something, and I thought that was best. Was it? Of course not, it was the worst thing I could have done, and for that, I'm sorry. When I met Tara, things fell into place, and she was able to fill in where I failed. I'm not good at this emotional stuff, son."

What an understatement, but it was a problem they both shared. Chris's rueful chuckle made his father laugh, too.

"Work was so important to me, I failed to realize how much you were hurting. I'm truly sorry, son. Can you forgive me?"

"It has been horrible for me." Part of him didn't want to forgive, but holding onto the anger would only hold him down. He sighed. "But I forgive you. I guess now I have to decide if I want to let Aaliyah into my life or not."

"Have you decided anything?" his father asked.

"I don't know… With what you and Tara have told me, I have to consider what's best for me and Aaliyah. I need more time to decide, but I'll get back to you, and Aaliyah."

"I'm proud of you, son. That sounds very reasonable to me." His father wrapped his arm around Chris's shoulders.

"Aaliyah also mentioned wanting to see Kanene, too. I haven't answered her about that either, because I'm not sure what to say."

His father shook his head. "Absolutely not. Kanene doesn't know who Aaliyah is. She only knows Tara as mum. I'm not having two confused children over Aaliyah's choices to leave the family. You now know what Aaliyah did to us was horrible, and I'm sorry again for my contribution to the problem, but, Christopher, there's one thing you need to know." Hugh embraced his son again. "You have a huge family who loves you. And no matter what you decide to do with Aaliyah in the future, we're not going anywhere."

"I know. Thanks, dad." Chris wrapped his arms around his father's waist.

"I probably don't say this often enough, but I'm proud of you, son. You're one hell of a kid."

Chris chuckled. "Thanks, dad. I love you."

"I love you, too, Christopher."

Chris held his father's gaze, but his thoughts drifted back to Alice. *If only she and I could talk like this, we could work out our problems. What am I going to do? How can I get her to open up to me?*

CHAPTER 15

The chiming of my mobile jerked me from my dream. I had been modeling alongside a surfboard, holding the cup for Edgington College for winning the Winter Swimming competition. I read the text message from Layla.

"Hello Alice! My clothing designer friend is going to drop by today. Please give him whatever he wants."

I dropped the mobile and buried my face beneath the sheets. "More men! If only they'd pay me, and let me be." I threw off the bedcovers and walked to the full-length mirror, hanging on the wall to the right of the bedroom door. "Let them pay you for the way you look, and no one will ever touch you again. Then, you can leave this place and get on with your life."

Strolling through the flat, I wiped down the worktops, dusted, and washed dishes in the sink. Another text message from Layla read she didn't care about how the flat appeared as long as her clothing designer friend liked me, but I wanted it to look nice.

The smell of bangers and mash, what I ate for dinner last night, lingered in the air. I listened to the news and muttered about politics

My hand trembled when I lit a match for a candle to freshen the room.

Why wasn't Layla coming with this designer to see me? Since I worked for her, you'd think she'd take an interest.

Ignoring my queasy stomach, I went to the bathroom and changed out of my T-shirt and shorts.

"He just wants to look at your bone structure," I said to my reflection, running a comb through my curls. "He's checking your measurements to make sure his designs fit you. Layla's at the shop. She said she trusts this guy, so you should, too. Layla hasn't lied before."

I put on lipstick and gazed at my reflection. Standing alone, I didn't mind the short, black dress.

While straightening the bedcovers, my mobile rocketed from my shaking fingers. Another text message from Layla.

"Make sure the clothing designer gets everything he asks for!"

Her original text message that awoke me from my dreams this morning had said the same thing…and yesterday at the shop… and now? I stared again at the text message.

"Whatever he asks for" had been written in all capital letters. I could almost hear Layla shouting at me to obey this unknown man's unspoken wishes.

Or demands… The thought made my stomach roll.

I walked into the kitchen, clutching the mobile in my trembling hand. *What does this clothing designer want from me?*

Unsettled by a sharp pang of fear, the urge to cry overwhelmed me. I set the mobile down and tried to strike a match to light another candle, but my entire body shook from the adrenaline rocketing through my body.

"Cool down, Alice. You've had some bad people in your life so far. It can't always be like that, have a bit of faith." I fumbled for a new match, fighting the old feelings.

After two more failed attempts at striking a match, I finally caught the wick on fire. I dashed to the bathroom and knelt over the toilet to vomit.

My head spun, but I brushed my teeth.

A knock sounded at the door. I clutched my stomach and pursed my lips.

"This is different," I told my pounding heart. "It's not Miguel."

I finally found enough courage to open the door. Layla's clothing-designer-friend stood just outside in a suit and tie, smiling down at me.

"Hello, pleased to meet you. I heard you're going to be my model. Aren't you going to invite me in?" He placed a firm hand on my shoulder. It was all I could do, not to burst into tears and run to the bathroom.

My thoughts circled as did the contents of my stomach, but Layla had told me to give him what he asked. I motioned him into the flat and stepped back.

The man pulled me into an embrace and shut the door behind me. No matter how I tried to convince myself this would be different, the touch of the man's smooth skin against mine inundated every sensation.

"So, Layla says this is your first time?" the man said.

My eyes widened. "First time, for what? Modeling? Yes." I looked up, needing comforting confirmation, but his black eyes gave me none.

The man chuckled. "Oh, no, not modeling, darlin'." He gestured toward the open bedroom door. "I'm talking about what's going to happen in there."

My stomach somersaulted and clenched into a knot, but I kept my expression neutral. This couldn't be happening—not again. My mind flashed back to the last time Miguel attacked me.

"Wh…what? I'm sorry, did you say…"

He nodded, a confident smirk on his face.

"I'm sorry, sir. I don't think Layla would—"

"Nonsense, darlin'. She said you'd give me whatever I wanted. And you are what I want." He ran his hands along my neck. I clamped my mouth shut, my pulse thundering in my ears. I'd had enough experience with Miguel to know overpowering him to escape wasn't possible.

"If—if this is what you want. I suppose I could give you that." My words sounded distant in my ears.

"Brilliant." The man chuckled and led me to the bedroom. "Don't worry, darlin'. I'll go easy on you, today." He lifted me and laid me on the bed.

Paralyzed, I couldn't move or speak. The horror that plagued me with Miguel was back, but with a stranger. The man started to undress. I shut my eyes, the crippling anxiety overtaking my mind.

Not again! I thought these people were going to help me, but I'm just a pawn in their sick game of life. They're going to work me to death. Goodbye college, friends, Jack, Christopher, and life as I knew it. I'm now a slave to the Dwight's, a slave in the worst way possible.

Lifted up again, I opened my eyes. He set me on my feet and nodded toward the bathroom. "Why don't you go and take your clothes off? I'll get things ready here."

Numb inside, I walked to the bathroom. Once I shut the door, anger surged through my veins. I ripped off my dress. I wanted to beat the hell out of the man who waited for me on the other side of the door. However, to find a solution to the mess I was in, I would have to get through him. Only then could I start forming a plan to get myself out of this new nightmare.

I wrapped my body in a towel and walked back to the bed, determined to hold onto the numbness inside me. Dropping the towel on the floor, I climbed beneath the bedcovers. The stranger beside me picked up the remote control on the bedside table and pushed a button to dim the lights.

When his time was finished, he thanked me and let me go. I jumped out of the bed, grabbed the towel, and walked to the bathroom. Shutting the door, I locked it and pulled my dress on.

Alice, why did you let it happen again? You could have told him you were ill. He might have let you go. Why didn't you fight, Alice? You're so useless. You've got to stand up for yourself. Nobody's going to do it for you.

I emerged from the bathroom on trembling legs. The so-called clothing designer was dressed. He placed an envelope on the kitchen table, but stopped at the door to smile.

"That was excellent. I will request you again. I'm telling Andrew, you're the girl for me. Thanks."

My face lost all colour. "I'm sorry, sir. Who is Andrew?"

"Sorry, I meant Edward Dwight. I think that's the name he's been using, right? You're lucky he really likes you. The other girls weren't as lucky."

"Wait, what other girls?" I clenched my hands together.

"Did you think you were the only girl, love?"

I nodded and the clothing designer stepped toward me. He placed his hands on my shoulders, caressing them. "Trust me, you're not the only one, but I'd appreciate it if you kept all of this between us."

I lost the ability to speak or move, hot blood surging through my frozen limbs. What were the Dwights thinking?

"The other girls were in a different block of flats, in a terrible part of town. They didn't have anything like this place. This was years ago." He ran a warm finger across my neck. My skin stung where he touched. "You're very lucky that the Carsons—uh... Dwights like you so much."

All I could do was nod. He led me to the door and bent down to kiss me on the cheek. "I'll see you tomorrow, darlin'."

I forced a smile, deadbolting the door behind him.

Enveloped by the scent of orange in the bedroom, I stumbled to the wardrobe for another look at the wardrobe. The extensive inventory made my stomach knot.

So this is why Edward and Layla, or whatever their names are, brought the clothes here. They weren't being nice to me...

An employee brought the clothes over while we took pictures at The Coral Clover, on the first day I had modeled. But in my ecstasy of new-found freedom, I lost all judgement of caution. I should have questioned their generosity more, especially with the sheer abundance of free everything they had thrown at me.

I hopped in the shower, letting the warm water wash the filth, guilt, and shame away. I wanted to curl up in a ball and die. This life wasn't worth living another second. I couldn't even look at myself in the mirror. I was worthless, a chewed up piece of chewing gum that nobody would love.

I'm going to end up alone for the rest of my life. I'm trapped again. I've been used and lied to by more adults. Why won't anyone help me get out of this cycle? I can't do it on my own, and now Edward and Layla are going to use me to make more money so they can afford more rubbish that they don't need. I can't believe Edward and Layla lied to me! It's not fair! I'm doing the best I can, but it's not good enough! It's never good enough. I'm not good enough. I want to die. Lord, please get me out of this living hell, it's not right. Nobody should ever endure it.

Tears poured down my cheeks. I longed for Chris, even my father. I should have tried harder with both of them, rather than keeping them at arms' length. If only one of them would come and save me from this nightmare I was trapped in. Picking up a razor, the thought of cutting myself crossed my mind, but I couldn't go through with it. Somehow, I had to find the mental strength to survive another day.

The sound of someone sliding a key in the lock and opening the front door brought me back to reality.

Edward's voice echoed through the flat. "Alice, it's Edward. Are you here?"

My heart thundered in my chest, a choking gasp and sniff my reply. Edward stepped into the bathroom. His smile evaporated when his eyes landed on my face.

"Alice, sweetie. What happened?"

I couldn't believe his green eyes had the audacity to still be sparkling. I sobbed, unable to stop myself. "What's your real name?"

"What are you talking about, love? It's Edward."

"Enough with the lies." I gasped for breath. "That guy who just left kept calling you Andrew. He also called your surname Carson. I'm not stupid, Edward—or whatever your name is. What's going on?" I yelled.

"I knew we shouldn't have trusted that man. Layla thinks the world of him, but he can't keep a secret to save his life. Come here, darling." He pulled on my wrist, his grip so firm I had no choice but to fall into his chest. I cried ever harder, being forced again to suffer another man's nearness.

"You're right, I am not Edward Dwight." He pushed my chin up until I looked into his eyes. "No, my name is Andrew Carson, but my wife is Layla, so you weren't lied to about everything."

And somehow that made it better? "Andrew, I can't do this. I want out. You have to let me go." I tried to step away but Andrew held me where I stood.

"Why?" He plucked a tissue from the dispenser on the counter and wiped the tears from my cheeks. "You've got it a lot better here than living with your mother and your despicable step-father." He caressed my shoulder. "You should also remember this, Alice..." His hands moved behind my head to grab my hair tight, the same way Miguel did. "If you leave, I'll kill Krisany."

Blood drained from my face despite Andrew's smile. He slid his hands down my back and rubbed. "Now, let me run and pick up some groceries for you." He bent and kissed me on the cheek, and walked out of the flat.

In the bathroom mirror a ghost white reflection stared back at me. I pressed my clenched fists against my cheeks.

I finally get away from my mother and her husband, thinking everything is going to be fine, and now... This!

Edward Dwight's true identity jogged another thought in my mind.

I should have listened to Jack, but I was too drunk at Beatrice's wedding to know what the hell was going on. It was all too good to be true. Andrew is going to work me to death.

CHAPTER 16

Chris walked down a corridor of Edgington, searching every space but giving smiles and friendly hellos to the fellow students he passed. He came upon Lisi and Kariann, deep in conversation. When their gaze shifted to him, they frowned.

"Hey, girls. What's up?" he asked.

"Have you heard from Alice?" Kariann ran a hand through her wet, dark-brown hair, her eyes welling with tears. "She wasn't in swim class this morning."

"No, I was coming to ask you the same thing. I haven't heard from her in days." Chris looked down at Lisi, who couldn't pull her mobile out of her backpack fast enough. "She told me she has a job, but I'm starting to worry because she has disappeared…" Distracted by Lisi's trembling hands trying to hold onto her mobile, he had to ask, "Lisi, are you all right?"

"No." Lisi bit her bottom lip and started typing, frantically. "My mum's terrified, too."

Her mobile chimed with an incoming text message.

"Where's D.J.?" Chris's innocent question only got him a glare from Kariann. Were the two siblings fighting again?

"He's on his way," she said, flatly.

Luke came down the corridor smiling. He stopped beside Lisi and started playing with her hair. She jerked her head up and glared at him.

Luke pursed his lips, but ran his fingers on the skin of her neck instead. "Am I in trouble?"

"No, would you please stop that." Lisi jerked away from him. "We've got a situation."

"Oh, what's going on?" Luke lowered his arm and clasped his hands together in front of him.

"Nobody's heard from Alice," Chris said.

"Are you serious?" Luke said, his eyes widening.

"Yeah." Chris frowned at his friend. How could he be this oblivious? "We're worried she might be in trouble."

"Lisi, do you know what's going on with Alice?" Kariann said. "You're the closest to her out of all of us."

That's right! Chris turned his intense stare on Lisi.

"I can't tell you." She shifted her weight from foot to foot, fidgeting with her mobile. "Alice doesn't want other people to know."

"Lisi, if Alice is in trouble, you've got to tell us." Luke rubbed her shoulders. "We can help her."

Lisi shook her head and ran down the corridor. The others followed Chris as he chased after her, dodging others in the way. Lisi barreled into the unaware D.J., but he still managed to wrap his arms around her to keep them both from falling.

"Whoa, Lisi. You all right?" He tried to peel her off him, but she buried her face into his shirt and clung to him. D.J. sighed. "I guess there's still no word from Alice."

Lord, I need some coffee right now. Why couldn't Alice send someone a text message.

"Lisi," Luke said, pulling his girlfriend out of D.J.'s arms. "What do you know about Alice?"

"Alice's parents treat her really bad." Lisi fell into Luke's chest, soaking his shirt instead.

"How so?" Kariann fingered a multi-coloured seashell bracelet on her wrist.

Sniffing several times, Lisi lifted her head to look at the group. "Her step-father beats her."

Luke put an arm around Lisi while others gasped. The group's shocked expression fell on Chris, but he'd never been an actor so he didn't bother trying to act surprised. He shrugged his shoulders and nodded.

"I knew it," Kariann said.

"We could go bash him up," D.J. said, folding his arms across his chest.

Chris shook his head, doubting that kind of action would fix anything. If only Alice had trusted him enough to ask him for help.

Lisi pulled away from Luke, throwing her arms around Chris's waist. "I'm scared, Chris." She now cried into his chest, ruining his shirt as well.

Chris sighed and hugged her back. "I'm scared, too."

Kariann stepped toward her brother, her eyes brimmed with tears and her bottom lip quivering.

"Come here." D.J. pulled his sister close.

Lifting her head, Kariann looked up at her brother's face, tears streaming from her eyes. "I wish I would have asked Alice about the bruises. But I just ignored it, and believed her story."

"It's okay. We'll find her." D.J. said, giving Kariann another squeeze. "If anyone hears from Alice, send a group text message so we know what's going on."

Everyone in the group murmured agreement.

"Lisi, there has got to be more to Alice's story than her stepfather beating her. Do you know anything else?" Luke may have asked the question to Alice's best friend, but it was Chris's gaze he held.

Chapter 17

I awoke to a text message from Layla. I wouldn't be allowed to go to Edgington today. I would be staying in the flat to take numerous men throughout the day. My stomach knotted at the thought of the upcoming task. I was in trouble.

Not even an hour later, Layla phoned me to ensure I was staying in the flat. Between bites of toast and orange marmalade, I asked if I could ever leave.

"You can leave when you've made us enough money. It shouldn't be more than a few weeks."

"Okay," I said through a mouth full of toast, though my eyes stung with building tears.

I hung up the mobile without another word and sat back in the chair. Revolted by the situation, I longed to tear myself apart. I didn't want to be used like this anymore. So much had been stolen away from me, I couldn't even look at myself in the mirror.

What they're doing is not right, and I'm not the only one. It's happening all around, but, somehow, nobody notices. Without help I'm going to forever be a victim, just like the others.

I took a long shower, trying to luxuriate in the sweet-smelling soaps and shampoo, before I would be used like a piece of crumpled paper. I dressed in a coral tank top and Levi shorts and looked at the clock. I was missing swim class.

"I won't miss practice tomorrow. You bloody people can't run my life."

I had a strict, six-day swim practice regiment, and I wasn't about to let Andrew and Layla ruin it for their selfish desires. Only practice would ensure I got a good ranking for Edgington in the Autumn Swimming Gala. We were on track to be in the top three. I longed for first place.

My mobile interrupted my thoughts about missing swim class. A text message from Chris.

"Oh great, what do you want now Christopher?" I muttered, walking away from the kitchen table with my mobile.

"Alice, where are you? I'm worried about you. Are you okay?"

I let out a mirthless laugh. "Yeah, sure, Chris. I'm all right. I'm being held against my will and they won't let me leave. I certainly have the time to tell you all about it." I continued muttering, writing a reply to his message, explaining I was in a predicament and I needed Lisi to call me when she had a chance.

Chris instantly responded. He wasn't happy.

Why can't I tell you what's going on? Because you should already know. Haven't I told you enough about my life to figure this out? Just stop texting me all the time, boy. It's getting on my nerves.

Sighing, I glared at the mobile and wrote a very rude reply. But, not wanting to cause another fight between Chris and myself, I erased the response and wrote another one. I really did want to tell Chris everything, but I didn't want to endanger him. With help from Lisi's mum, I hoped to get out of this. I could come clean to Chris later.

I sat on the settee with my knees pulled up to my chest and let my mind wander. The only sound was the clock ticking next to the flat screen television, on the wall opposite me.

Alice you've got to get out of this. You can run. It's not like Andrew or Layla are watching you. Hmm, maybe there's something in the cupboards that can help me escape.

I opened the kitchen cupboards and looked through their contents—nothing but plates, pots, pans, and cutlery.

Inside the refrigerator, I found a bottle of scotch. *Perfect!* I reached into one of the cupboards and pulled out two glasses. I set everything on the table and smiled down at the bottle of scotch.

"Since I don't have a gun, the least I can do is make you drunk, you little thug." I replaced the bottle in the refrigerator and slammed the door.

A box of matches sat next to an orange candle on the worktop. I struck a match and watched the golden flame dance on the end. Smoke filled the air as I neared the glowing mass to the candle's wick. The candle turned to liquid in the jar, creating a strong smell of orange that wafted through the air.

Breathing in the scent of orange slowed my thudding heart. My mobile chimed with a text message from Layla. My heart sank, spreading a cold throughout my body. The man was coming up to the flat. My stomach, already tightened in knots, sent toast up my esophagus. I rushed to the toilet and vomited.

After brushing my teeth, I looked in the mirror. Bloodshot eyes glared back against ghost white features. My entire body shook from head to foot. Unable to gulp more than shallow breaths, I struggled to breathe.

At the knock on the door, I swished mouthwash and counted slowly to calm my breathing.

My legs moved like they weighed fifty pounds, each slow step inching me closer to my doom. I furiously rubbed my stomach, trying to chase the knots away. Sweat, as cold as ice, continued trickling down my neck and back. Standing in front of the door, I slipped my mobile into my short's pocket. Slowly, I reached out with trembling hands and unlocked the door.

A lorry driver stepped over the threshold, his caramel-blond hair slicked down over his forehead. "Hello, sweet'art. I hear you're mine for the next hour. Jolly good!"

My numb tongue refused to work, my mouth hot and dry as the desert on a summer's day. An overreaction wouldn't help me escape, so I played along, nodding and shutting the door behind him.

His dark eyes scanned the room before resting on me. I tensed, watching his gaze travel from my head to my feet and back, to linger on my chest.

"I like to know what I'm working with sweet'art. Let's have a look?" Smiling, he reached toward my bare shoulders.

No, no, no, this can't be happening again! I fought the urge to scream and fight like hell, but Andrew's threat to kill Krissy kept me inside this prison. I couldn't endanger Krisany, no matter how bad things got for me. I wouldn't betray her after everything she had done for me over the years. She'd saved my life in too many ways.

Be strong for Krissy, you can do it.

He pulled me into a tight embrace. "Are you nervous?" he asked, running his roughened fingers along my face.

"No." I cleared my throat and glanced toward the refrigerator. "Would you like a drink before we get started?"

"Awe, that's brilliant—setting the mood." He gazed down at me, his hands caressing all the way down to my lower back. "You're beautiful." He stole a kiss and walked us to the table.

Once he sat, I moved to the refrigerator and quickly pulled out the bottle of scotch. "How's this?"

He flashed gleaming teeth to my question, his eyes dancing from the scotch in my white-knuckled grip to my face.

"Do you want yours neat or on the rocks," I asked, squeezing the bottle's neck tighter to hide my trembling hands.

"Neat." He smiled.

Pouring him a glass, I struggled not to gag at the oaky smell, but his dark eyes watched every move I made.

Lord, help me. I sauntered closer, holding out his drink as far as my arm would extend. *You disgusting man, I wish I had a hammer.*

Flashing me another smile, he took the glass but clasped my now free fingers in his other hand. "Thanks, sweet'art!" He downed a large portion of the liquid, but still did not let me go. *Stop touching me, you disgusting freak.* "Oh, I still need to pour mine," I said with a laugh.

Nodding, he let go, but his calloused fingers left behind a residual sensation on my skin. I forced my smile to remain broad and walked back to the refrigerator. I pulled out ice and dropped it into the second glass before pouring more scotch. I hoped the added ice would hide how little I poured for myself. I wanted him drunk, not me.

I made a point to sit on the other side of the table, but made sure to bat my eyelashes at the lorry driver so he wouldn't notice the distance. Taking a sip, I let the scotch run down my throat—it warmed my shaking, frozen limbs.

His stare seemed to be undressing me, but maybe a little conversation would distract him.

"So, where are you from?" I asked, putting the glass on the table.

"I've lived in Shiremoor my whole life. I've been out of school for a year. I support myself by driving a lorry."

My mind ground to a halt. This guy was only a year older than me, but he looked like he was thirty-years-old. I clenched my hands on my shaking legs and studied the lorry driver's face. "What got you interested in seeing girls like this?" Wait! I shouldn't have asked that, not if I wanted to keep his thoughts away from why he was here. I wiped the sweat from my clenched hands on my shorts.

The lorry driver emptied his glass and set it on the table. "I've known Andrew Carson for a few years. He mentors me on some business stuff. One day, he told me about his girls. I went, and now I go quite frequently. So, shall we get started?"

I knew it! I should have never asked the question. What do I do now?

The man stepped behind me and rested his hands on my shoulders. He bent, resting his smooth chin against my neck. "Right. Let's get on with it sweet'art," he whispered in my ear.

His hands snaked beneath my shirt, his roughened fingers reaching around for my breast.

I bolted out of the chair and spun toward him. It's not like he wouldn't try again, but at least my actions bought me more time to think.

His hot breath ran along my collar bone, his mouth making a trail of kisses that ended at my lips.

I didn't recoil. I needed to play the part in full, though my mind frantically sought for a way to diffuse the situation from going further. He sighed against my lips and pulled me off my feet. I wrapped my legs around his waist to counter my sudden shift in balance. He groaned and deepened the kiss. I pulled at his golden hair, but he only seemed to like it more, shoving his tongue deep into my mouth.

The smell of scotch and cologne filled my nostrils. I found myself relaxing in his embrace.

Don't you dare. What the hell are you doing? He's using you. Get ahold of yourself, Alice!

Breathing deeply, he set me on the ground. His eyes held a fire now and a triumphant smile.

"Wow, sweet'art, you're a damn good kisser, you know that?" He ran his fingers through my wet hair.

"No, I'm…"

His arms slid down my back in such a sensual way my voice failed. He pressed his lips to mine once more. "Let me have a look," he said, his gaze sliding down to my chest.

"Okay." I swallowed the lump clogging my throat. "But how about another drink, first." It was such a lame excuse he might not go for it, but I couldn't think of anything else.

His hands stopped caressing my back and he nodded. "If it'll help you loosen up, why not?"

"Great. Wait here." Though my heart raced, I forced my steps to remain unhurried as I walked over to the table.

A mobile rang.

"I'll just be a moment." He pulled a mobile from his pocket and walked over to the large window in the lounge.

I took his distraction as a blessing and poured an even larger amount of scotch into his glass. It wasn't long before the lorry driver's arm snaked around my middle, pulling my backside into him. He took the glass in my hand and downed the contents. I smiled, his action working in my favour.

He forced me to face him, but his glazed-over expression already showed signs of being drunk. "Kiss me...again."

His slurred words gave me the confidence to lean in. Now I was in control.

"That's it." He placed his hands on the back of my head, holding me captive with our lips locked. So much for being in control.

I had to act fast, feeling his hands at the top of my shorts and his roughened fingers tracing my bare skin. I jerked my head to the side to break the kiss. "Hey, I forgot to choose an outfit," I said, the side of my face buried in his sweat-soaked T-shirt. "Want to pick your favourite?"

"Really?" he slurred, his hands trying to push my shorts down though he still hadn't undone the button to loosen them from my hips.

"Sure, love," I said with as much enthusiasm I could muster. "I like you."

"I like you, too," he whispered, the smell of scotch overwhelming.

He held onto my shoulders, staggering behind me to the wardrobe. I helped him look through the numerous lingerie items

Layla had left for me. He found a dressing gown in ivory silk and handed it to me.

"Here sweet'art. While you...I'm going to..." He stumbled away, going toward the settee.

"That's fine." I waited until he sat down and pulled out his mobile, then headed to the bathroom. I took one last look before closing the door. Slumped over, he looked like he would hurt himself if he moved without help. I hope he stayed that way.

I turned on the tap of the bath, hoping the noise would cancel out my voice. I unlocked my mobile and scrolled through my contacts. My eyes fell on Chris's name. Such a strong assurance came over me, I tapped on his number.

"Hello," he said, quickly.

"Chris," I whispered, pressing the mobile closer to my face. I hadn't heard any sound outside the bathroom for so long, I took a chance and peaked out. The lorry driver held his head in his hands. His head snapped up, his gaze locking on me.

"Hey, what are you doing in there? I can't wait on you any longer."

"Who was that?" Chris asked. "What does he want?"

The man stood, but fell back onto the settee. I shut and locked the door, then crumpled to the floor. "It's a lorry driver. Chris, I'm stuck here." I kept my back pressed to the door and drew my knees toward my chest. "If my plan doesn't work, I don't know what I'm going to do."

"Alice, what do you mean you're stuck. Why weren't you in swim class or chemistry today?"

"They won't let me leave. I've got a plan to escape, but I'm not sure it's going to work."

"Who won't let you leave?"

"Andrew and his wife." I pressed my ear to the door, relieved the man hadn't started pounding on the other side.

"Who's Andrew?" Chris said.

"My mum's friend, the one I met at her wedding."

"Is Andrew the person you've been hanging with the last few weeks?" He sounded incredulous.

"Yes, but it wasn't like this at first. He's doing some pretty bad things to me." I cried, wishing I could have kept this truth from him. He would probably never look at me the same.

"Is the lorry driver who just yelled at you involved?"

"Yes." I sniffed. I needed to calm down or nothing I did would help me.

Chris's voice turned gruff. "I'm coming to get you, tell me where you are."

"No, I can't. I don't want to endanger you."

"Then you've got to call the police."

"No way!" I exclaimed. "If the police get involved, Andrew will kill me."

Chris let out a long and loud sigh. "Fine. What's your plan?"

"I got the lorry driver to drink some scotch, he's pretty drunk but still conscious. I'm thinking about making a cocktail using one of the sleeping pills I stole from my mum's house to knock him out. But once he comes too, he'll still tell Andrew, so I'm not sure if I should even try."

"Alice, it's a good plan, but I would still call the police. Make it look like he's been trespassing and rifling through your stuff. They'll haul him off to jail, where he can't call Andrew."

"That's a good idea." I shivered.

"You're very clever. You can pull this off," he said, enthusiastically.

"Really? Thank you, you've never said so before."

He sighed. "That's because you haven't been open to me, love. I had no idea what was going on, and now that I do, your behavior makes sense."

"Chris, I didn't tell you because I worried you would run away." I wiped at the fresh tears falling from my eyes. "Nobody's ever stuck by me, except Lisi and her mum. I've been living in a nightmare my entire life. And now I'm in a new one."

"Alice, it's going to be okay. Why don't you meet me at Biscuits and Confetti after you escape, and we'll figure out together what to do from there."

"No, I can't go there." I said the words so loudly I cringed. I took a deep breath and whispered, "It's right next door to a clothing boutique owned by Andrew's wife, Layla."

"She owns Coral Clover?"

"Yes." I sniffed a few times.

"Hmm...I have an idea." The confidence in Chris's tone helped strengthen my resolve to go through with the plan. "Wait in the flat for me. I'll pick up my car and meet you there."

I let out a broken laugh and tried to compose myself. "I suppose I could do that, but what if someone else comes up? What do I do?"

"I know, text me Andrew's number. I'll let him know I'm looking for a girl right away."

"All right. Do our friends know what's going on?" I asked, my fingers tightening around my mobile.

"They know your step-father beats you and that you're missing, but they don't know about this." He sounded so hesitant, I doubted he had been the one to tell them.

"Did Lisi tell them?"

He sighed. "Yes. Everyone was so terrified that something happened to you, she told them about your step-father."

I heard the school bell jangle. "Oh, you're still at Edgington."

"It's okay. I'm coming for you. Text me the second that guy is out of the flat so I know you're safe."

"Okay, thanks. I'll see you soon." I hung up the mobile and placed it in my pocket. Turning off the tap, I threw on the dressing gown over my clothes.

Opening a drawer, I took out the package of sleeping pills I stole from Beatrice and Miguel. I dumped one into my hand and closed the drawer. Unstopping the drain, I listened to the flowing water.

Here goes nothing. I clenched the pill in my fist. Lord, please let me get away from Andrew Carson. Please let me live!

I stepped out of the bathroom and turned off the light. The man lay on the settee. I couldn't tell if his eyes were open, but he didn't try to move when I shut the bathroom door. I left the water to drain and walked to the kitchen table.

Picking up his empty glass, I poured another drink. At the sound of movement behind me, I quickly dropped the pill into the liquid. I didn't know how fast it would dissolve so I tossed an ice cube in, too. I glanced over my shoulder. He had opened his eyes, but they still looked heavy.

"I'm just mixing you one more drink before we begin, love." I grabbed a spoon and did my slowest meander toward the settee while stirring. I had no idea if all evidence of the pill would be gone by then. I had never tried to drug anybody before.

The lorry driver ripped the drink out of my hand—not even bothering to look at it before downing it. He tried to glance up at me, but his drooping eyelids didn't get much past my waist. He slumped over the armrest and the glass in his hand clanked to the floor.

The moment I was sure he slept, I rushed to the wardrobe. I threw the dressing gown to the floor and pulled clothing items off hangers. Tossing them everywhere as I went into the bedroom. I knocked down a box of seashells and a vase of fresh flowers, leaving the water to saturate the carpet. I opened the bedside table drawers and knocked over both lamps. I even tossed the bedcovers to the floor. I returned to the lounge to find the driver still asleep. I smiled. My plan had worked. There was only one thing left to do.

Standing in the corridor, outside the flat, I called the police. "There's a burglar in my flat. I think he found my parents' scotch in the refrigerator. He's passed out on the settee."

Within minutes, the police arrived. A female detective made sure I was all right while two male officers went into the flat and arrested the lorry driver.

Drunk and groggy, he couldn't answer the simplest of questions, not even his name. They placed him in handcuffs and led him out of the flat. To my relief, he didn't look at me when he passed.

After assuring the officers I wasn't hurt and would be fine, now that the intruder was gone, I went back in the flat and locked the door.

"Thank you, Chris, for your help." I texted. "He's gone."

It took a lot of work to clean up the disaster I had made. Layla called in the middle of it all.

"Did my client leave satisfied?"

"Yes," I said. "He got a little too rough and messed up the place, but I'm taking care of it."

"Are *you* all right?"

"Oh, yes." I forced a laugh. I didn't need her coming over here to check on me. "I'm just going to need some time to get this place back together."

"Fine. I'll block out the rest of the schedule until the afternoon. There's a young man who insisted upon coming. He even paid double."

She hung up without even a goodbye, but I didn't care. I turned on the music on my mobile and sang my way through the chores. I was on my way out of the second nightmare of my life. I had to focus on the happiness—not the thought of Andrew and Layla coming after me once they discovered I lied to them. Staying frozen in fear would accomplish nothing.

Chapter 18

Chris walked through the foyer toward the lift bank, lost in thought.

I'm going to the police, no matter what she says. I've got to tell them what's going on, even if she doesn't want me to say anything. I must protect Alice. I wish I could beat Andrew up myself, but I'll let the police handle that.

Inside the flat, Chris watched Alice gather clothes into her backpack. She stopped packing to run to the bathroom. She returned with a package of sleeping pills that she threw on top of her packed clothes.

Someone pounded on the door.

A male voice yelled from the outside. "Shiremoor Police!"

Alice's face turned white, her eyes as big as dinner plates. Alice backed toward the bedroom window.

Chris cocked his head. "Why are the police here?"

"They're probably here for me. We've got to get out of here." Alice heaved on the window's frame, but it didn't budge.

"Why? Let's tell them what's going on." It was the perfect opportunity. They could protect her better than he could.

"Andrew wasn't the only one that was doing illegal things, Chris. I could be in trouble." She finally realized she needed to unlock the window's latch and it raised up. "Either come with me or I'll get out of here without you."

Chris squelched a sigh. *You can't make this easy, can you babe? Well, here we go then.*

He ran over and looked down. The fire escape was right below. "We've got five stories to go down. Do you trust me?"

Alice nodded.

He put his lips close to her ear. "Don't worry," he whispered, "I'll go first. Stay with me."

Alice didn't even hesitate. She inched forward right after Chris. The window's metal frame groaned under their weight.

A crash echoed through the flat. "Are you here, Miss Esposido? We have some more questions."

Chris furrowed his brows. "Esposido?"

"They needed a name. I couldn't use Lisi's, so I gave them Beatrice and Miguel's," Alice whispered.

"Oh, I see." He took great care to close the window as quietly as possible. It bothered him that she had never shared this simple part of her life with him before, but now was not the time to dwell on their lack of communication. They needed to get out of here. Each step they took down the fire escape brought metal scraping against stone. Frantic whispers between each step were all they had.

"You don't really think you're going to get arrested, do you?"

Alice pursed her lips, grabbed her backpack straps with both hands and took another step down. Metal clanged against the window ledge on the floor below. Chris grabbed her around the waist and pushed her against the wall.

"We're never going to get down like this." She pushed at his chest, pressed against hers. "Let me go, this is terrifying."

"We'll only make it down if we stay together. You can trust me, Alice." Chris took her hand, his thumb rubbing circles between her finger and thumb. "Come on." He tugged her into motion again, descending the fire escape. The way she kept biting her lower lip made her look so innocent and sweet.

"Are you sure you don't want to talk to the police?" he whispered, unable to stop himself from asking again.

Alice shook her head.

"All right."

The fire escape ladder ended ten feet above the ground. Chris pulled on her hand. He pointed at himself then at the ground. She nodded and took off her backpack. Chris climbed down to the end rung and dropped to the ground.

Alice stepped to the top of the ladder and crouched. "Terrific. What about me?"

"Toss me your bag."

She let it drop. "And now what?"

"Climb down." Chris held out his arms. "You can trust me, babe."

Alice sighed, but still climbed down to the lowest rung.

"Okay. Let go."

She closed her eyes and released one finger at a time. Chris stopped her plummet to the ground just like he promised.

"Thanks," she said with a half smile.

"You're welcome." Chris tightened his arms around her middle for just a reassuring second before letting her go.

They walked around to the front of the building. A police car sat outside.

"Where's your car?" Alice said.

"Next to the police car. This is not going to work. Hey, I saw a pub behind this building when I arrived. Let's go there."

"I know that place, it's called Keshmore's. If we take a right down this alley," she said, gesturing toward a strip of pavement between buildings, "we'll end up on the road behind the flats. We can walk to the pub."

"Brilliant."

Chris followed Alice down the alley, wrinkling his nose at the smell of rubbish. Reaching the street, they walked toward the entrance of Keshmore's Pub. Only a short queue of people stood outside, but Alice tensed as they drew near.

"What's wrong, Alice?"

She pointed to the security guard standing outside.

"You'll be all right." Chris placed an arm around her shoulders. "I won't let anything happen to you. Come on, love." He inched her forward by patting her bare shoulder.

"Hello there, may I see some identification?" The security guard said, his black T-shirt and Levi shorts clinging to his muscular body. His smile didn't seem menacing, but the way he folded his arms did make his arms bulge. This wasn't a man to be messed with lightly.

"Hello, sir. Yes, we do have identification," Chris said, handing him his driving license. He nudged for Alice to retrieve hers, but Alice didn't move.

"Thank you, sir. Uh...is she all right?" The security guard narrowed his eyes at Alice's pale complexion.

"Yes, she's having a rough day. Let me get her driving license," Chris said, unzipping Alice's backpack. He rummaged around for her wallet. "Here it is." He pulled out the wallet and handed it to the security guard.

Staring down at the license, the man's lips formed into a frown. Chris replaced his arm around Alice's shoulders and caressed her right shoulder. She leaned into his side, her body continuing to shake.

"You're only seventeen, young lady. You're not old enough to drink. Sir, did you know this?" The man held Chris's gaze.

He glanced down at the license. *Alice Julian?* He wasn't sure what was going on, but now was not the time to discuss it. "Uh... yes sir, I do. I'll make sure she doesn't have a drink. In fact, we dropped by for a glass of water. We've just come from the gym." Chris took the wallet and slid it into Alice's backpack and zipped it up.

The security guard looked back and forth between them. "I suppose I can let you get a glass of water, but nothing more—for either of you. I'm going to let my colleagues, Gordon and Monica, know to watch out for you two." He pulled out a mobile and unlocked it.

"That's fine," Chris said, watching the security guard type into the mobile.

"All right then, go on in." The man stepped to the side.

"Thank you, sir," Chris said with a smile.

Alice managed to finally find her voice. "Yes, thank you."

Chris steered her to the right and through the front doors. The bright room they entered had white walls and a brown tile floor. A man stood behind the bar. A long, black apron hung over his white T-shirt and jeans. The guy looked to be around six foot, and someone else Chris wouldn't want to start a fight with.

He wiped his hands on his apron and rounded the counter toward them. "Hello, you two. You're the kids I'm supposed to look after, eh?"

Chris and Alice nodded.

"Brilliant. I'm Gordon, nice to meet you. Come, sit, and I'll get you some water." He gestured to the bar behind him.

Alice and Chris sat on red, leather stools at the bar. It didn't take long for their glasses of water to arrive. They thanked Gordon and sipped their drinks.

"Alice, what's going on?" Chris whispered, leaning toward her.

Alice shook her head. "I'm not telling you a thing, especially when we're out here." She gestured around the room, filling with other patrons. "It's too dangerous, until we're hidden."

To their right, a cook and a girl clad in a wet apron carried trays full of food to serve to the patrons.

"Darling," Chris said, "where do you expect us to go? We can't get to my car it's—"

"I know, back there where the police are. But if we stay here, the police could find us, Christopher. I am not going with them." She folded her arms.

Chris sighed. They couldn't stay here forever. They needed to keep moving. He slid his stool closer to her and sat down. He pulled her into a one arm embrace and let his lips touch her ear. "Babe, you've got to tell me what's going on. I have no idea how to help you unless—"

Alice gasped and her eyes widened. "That's it," she whispered, turning her head to the swinging kitchen doors, which squeaked.

"What?"

"Come on, babe. Let's go," she said, sliding off her stool.

"Alice, what are you—"

"Shhh, quick, before anyone sees us." She grabbed his hand and pulled him through the doors. To her right another door sat ajar. She walked closer, pulling him along. It was a supply pantry. She ducked inside, taking Chris with her.

Chris shut the door and they stood in the silence, listening to the muffled sound of the cook returning to the kitchen—chattering, dishes being washed, and the sound of a spatula on the grill.

"Okay, Alice." Chris pulled out his mobile and turned on the torch. "Will you please tell me what's going on?"

"I can't." She walked away from him, but in the cramped space she couldn't get far.

"Why not?" Hadn't he done enough already to show that he could be trusted. "What could you possibly tell me that's worse than your step-father bashing you up?" He followed her, holding his mobile over her head to light up the tile floor ahead of them.

"Chris, it's not that simple. It's—" Her flailing hand hit a broom handle and it thudded against the pantry door on its way down.

Alice gasped and froze, but Chris moved into action. He grabbed her around the waist and led her to the empty corner ahead of them. She backed up until her backpack hit the wall.

"We can still be seen," she whispered, her eyes brimming with tears.

"Lay down," Chris said.

"What?"

"Lay down, Alice. These lower shelves here will hide us if we lay down."

"But—"

"Fine, I'll be on the floor." Chris laid his back on the cold tile and beckoned her to him. She bit her lip instead, tears falling down her face

"Alice, now." He did his best to keep his tone to a whisper, but it was hard with the urgency he felt.

Finally, she knelt next to him. It wasn't exactly what he asked for, but it was a start.

Chris turned off the torch and put the mobile back in his pocket. "Sweetheart, you need to—"

The doorknob rattled.

Alice gasped and climbed on top of Chris.

He slowly reached up and drew her head down to his chest. "Shhh, it's okay," he whispered.

Her body shook on top of him. He slid his hand under the bag resting on her back and locked them together. This close, the flowery scent of her still damp hair was impossible to ignore, or the way it had left the back of her shirt wet.

Oh, Lord, even in the dark she's beautiful. Don't get worked up over this, mate. Now is not the time to lose control.

Her heart raced against his chest, her fingers clinging to his shirt. The silence stretched on so long, Chris started to stroke her back. Her body began to relax beneath his fingers.

"Baby, what's going on?" he whispered. "I love you, but I can't help you if you don't tell me."

Her body jerked and a muffled sob went into his shirt.

"Sweetie, what is it?" Chris locked his fingers together again. He held her as close to him as possible. The nearness was almost more than he could bear. "Alice, I want you so bad, but I need to know what's been going on—all of it. Please let me in."

"If I tell you, you might not want me anymore."

"When are you going to finally trust me." He gave her a comforting squeeze with his arms. "Look at where we're at, what I've done. All of this is for you."

She pressed her lips to his, even as tears fell from her eyes. He forced his arms to relax, unsure of what this meant, but he didn't want to be accused of demanding more than she was willing to give. She broke the kiss and replaced her head on his chest.

"All right." She sniffed. "Besides, you already know my mum and step-father are mad."

The comment made an uncomfortable chuckle escape from him. He kissed the top of her head, hoping to assure her that he wasn't taking anything she said lightly.

"They've used drugs constantly throughout my life. I've been kicked out of my house so many times, I've lost count. I always stay with Lisi when they throw me out. If I didn't have her and her mum, I don't know where I would have gone. When I was eleven-years-old, Miguel started beating me. He did it whenever I didn't do what he wanted or he thought I misbehaved, which was all the time. Sometimes, I felt he did it out of pleasure for himself, because he knew I wouldn't fight back. If I did, he always got more violent toward me."

"What did your mum do?" Chris ran a finger along her quivering chin.

"She stood by and encouraged him."

"I hope they burn in hell for the way they've treated you," he said, wishing more than ever to get his hands on her parents. Someone needed to teach those monsters a lesson.

"That's not all." She sobbed, but the pantry door cracked open. She pressed her face into his shirt, muffling the sound.

Whoever it was lifted the broom off the floor and shut the door. He held his breath, wishing her sniffs weren't so loud, but nothing could be done about that.

"Shh, baby, it's all right." He rubbed her back in hopes to quell her shaking body. They would be found for sure if her crying got any louder.

Her head popped off his chest. "No, you need to know... Miguel has forced me to do things."

Chris's stomach knotted at the inudeno in her tone. "You mean like sexual things?"

She buried her face in his chest again. "I didn't dare tell you, because I thought you would run away."

Though his shirt muffled her voice, it wasn't enough that he didn't understand. "I won't run away, love."

"But it's been going on so long, since I was eleven, so I'm not as good as other girls." She moaned, replacing her head on his chest.

"Oh, good Lord." Chris was at a loss of what to say or do, but none of that mattered, she clung to him with all her strength.

"I thought Andrew and his wife were trying to help me get out of that situation, but it was a lie. They started sending strange men to my flat." She sobbed so hard her shoulders shook.

How could they do this to her? It's amazing she survived this long. It finally makes sense why she pulled away from me, especially when I kept getting angry. How did I miss this?

"Chris?" She sniffed. "Are you thinking about running away now?"

"No. You didn't do this. You've been manipulated and abused by adults your entire life, but I promise it won't happen anymore." He captured her cheeks in his hands. "I love you and I'll never leave you," he whispered.

She nodded and threw her lips against his. The salty taste of her tears kept him from losing control. She pulled away and sniffed. "Thank you for everything—though your parents might not be so happy if they ever find out how messed up I am."

"Not to worry. My family comes with issues, too," Chris said. "My biological mum ran out on the family. She wants to meet with me and talk about it, but I don't want to. I've got too much to worry about with graduating college, preparing for university, and spending time with my girlfriend…" He caressed the back of her neck, "…if she'll have me."

"I'm with you—wherever you want to go."

"Good, because I think we need to get out of here and get you to the police before this Andrew character shows up to check on you." He expected her to put up a fight, even if only a whispered one, but she didn't.

"Okay. But first, take me to Krissy."

"Krissy?" he said. "You mean Lisi's mum?"

Alice nodded her head, but stopped moving at the sound of a commotion in the kitchen. Chris lifted his head off the floor, listening to someone calling for help to stop a fight. "It sounds like they're distracted out there. Let's go." He only had to nudge a little to get her to stand. She even reached down and helped him up. He kept her hand firmly held in his, even after he was steady.

Easing back the pantry door, revealed the kitchen to be empty. "It's clear." He pulled her toward the open backdoor, right past the stove still warm from use.

The door led into a darkened alley behind the building that helped them circle back toward the front of the building where his car was parked. Thankfully, the police car was now gone.

"So, why are we going to Lisi's mum?" he said, hurrying toward his car with Alice's hand still in his.

"She's always there for me. She deserves to know what's going on, and she'll know what to do."

As long as it ended with Lisi's mum telling her to go to the police. It was the best course of action, if he was going to have any chance of protecting her.

CHAPTER 19

Sitting in the passenger's seat, I glanced at Chris, his face a glow from the car's display. "Thanks for taking me to Krissy's," I said, my nose still clogged from all my crying.

"Alice, are you sure you don't want to go to the police first? They can protect you better than any of us can."

"I haven't told you everything." I saw his grip on the steering wheel tighten at my words. I placed my hand on his shoulder. "Andrew said, if I went to the police, he would kill Krissy."

"What? How do they know each other?"

"From years ago—at university." I laced my fingers together and placed them on my knee.

"Don't you think it's risking a lot to go to Krissy's house, if Andrew said he's going to kill her?" Chris let off the accelerator.

"No, punch it," I said. "We need to get there as soon as possible. She needs to be warned about what's going on."

"But—"

"Christopher, I need Krissy's help. Where else am I supposed to go? I'm certainly not going back to Beatrice's." Just mentioning her name made a shiver run down my spine.

"Alice, you should go to the police. This is insane!"

"Please, Chris, I have to deal with this first. Just take me to Krissy's house." I folded my arms, digging my fingernails into my skin.

"Fine." He floored the accelerator and the car took off in earnest. Chris redirected a dashboard vent. Blasted by warm air, the warmth helped calm my shaking body. "You can turn the heat up if you want."

"Thanks, I guess." I said, flatly. Sighing, I glanced at Chris who gripped the steering wheel with both hands. "You don't know what my life has been like, Chris. I don't like you telling me what to do. Everyone else does that to me already."

Chris pulled the car to the side of the road and slammed on the breaks—bringing us to a grinding halt. Frozen by his unexpected action, I didn't fight him when he reached over and peeled my fingers off my left arm.

Taking my hand in his, he held it tight. "Alice, what do you want me to do?" His grip kept increasing until it became painful.

I ripped my fingers out of his grasp. "Chris, there's nothing you can do besides get me to Krissy, before Andrew and Layla try anything."

He sat still as a statue in the driver's seat. "You can rage at me all you want, but I don't care. I'm going to help you."

A frown grooved my mouth. "So, no matter how angry I get, it won't stop you from going to the police?" I wiped the sweat from our hands on my shorts.

"Nothing will stop me from saving your life," Chris said in a low voice.

"Then, I want you to take me to Krissy's house and leave me there. Do what you want, I can't stop you. But, if you call the police, I'll never speak to you again." The welling tears burned my already sensitive eyes. Why couldn't he see that going to the police put Krissy in greater danger?

His jaw clenched and he sighed. "All right." He pulled the car back onto the road, pushing the vehicle's speed to its very limits.

The remainder of the drive passed in silence, the tension between us thick and immovable. Chris wanted to be the hero, but I wanted to ensure Krisany's safety. She had always been there for me. I was not about to rely on a kid I barely knew.

The moment Chris parked in the driveway, I climbed out of the car. I ran up the stairs and swung the front door open, receiving exclamations of joy from Kahleesi and Serena who looked up from their homework. Krisany ran to the door and embraced me.

"I'm fine," I lied, pulling her into the kitchen. "Krissy, I need to talk to my dad." He had warned me about Andrew in the first place. He might be able to offer the best insights on how I could realistically deal with him, and keep everyone safe. "Do you think we could call him?" Krisany nodded and pulled her mobile out of her handbag. Tapping on the number for "Wandsworth Prison," she handed the mobile to me and left the room. I knew she and the girls wouldn't go far, listening to my one-sided conversation from the lounge.

"Wandsworth Prison, how may I direct your call?" a female voice asked.

"Hello, I'd like to speak to a prisoner." My voice shook and my heart pounded.

Jack, answer, please. I've got to talk to you.

"All right, Miss. Who is the prisoner you're trying to reach?"

"Jack Julian," I said, wiping the sweat from the crease of my arm.

"One moment please." The phone went to music, and a male voice listed rules for visiting the prison. I focused on trying to control my pounding heart, breathing in and out in a steady rhythm.

Jack please talk to me. Finally, the music stopped. I tensed in anticipation.

"Miss, are you still there?" the female voice asked.

"Yes." My voice croaked, my throat surprisingly dry.

"I'm sorry, but Mr. Julian has declined the call."

"Oh..." He couldn't even be bothered to listen to my plight? My world, and all its consequences, seemed to weigh even heavier, making it difficult to breathe. "Thank you," I whispered, my voice trembling.

"Of course, have a good evening," the woman said and hung up.

I let the mobile fall from my hand, onto the kitchen table. Turning away, I ran up the stairs and into the bedroom I used when I stayed at the house. Slamming the door, I dropped my backpack and flopped onto the bed. I buried my face in the pillows and fell to pieces.

Sobs racked my shaking body. I punched the pillows and bed repeatedly. "What am I going to do? I've got no one who will help me. Someone's going to die if I don't do something." I pressed my face again into the pillows. "I hope it'll be only me. I should have never been born."

CHAPTER 20

Inside the police station, Chris came face-to-face with the receptionist, her name tag said "Kolini".

Kolini's bleached-blonde straight hair flowed over her shoulders, her blue eyes, eyeing him with interest. A big nose dominated her face, and her high cheek bones made her mouth look as if it were in a flat line atop her pointed jaw, which added to the disproportionate facial structure.

"Hello, sir. What can I help you with?" Her tone sounded dismissive, but her slight smile encouraged Chris.

"Hello. I need to talk to someone. My girlfriend is in trouble." He still panted, having run all the way from the car park.

"Can I have more details to pass along?"

Chris opened his mouth to speak, but a bald, slender man, dressed in a police uniform, appeared from around the corner.

"Hello, son. My name is Detective McDonough. What can I help you with this evening?"

"Sir, my girlfriend is in great danger. We have to help her," Chris said, the urgency of the situation making his voice rise.

"All right, son. Follow me. We don't want a scene out here." Detective McDonough smiled in Kolini's direction. She nodded, allowing Chris to follow the detective down a corridor.

They entered a small room with a brown, round table. Two black, plastic chairs sat across from each other. Detective McDonough shut the door and motioned for Chris to take the chair in front of him.

Chris took it with a smile. "Thank you, sir."

"You're welcome. What is your name, son?" Detective McDonough retrieved a pad of paper and a pen from a worktop to the left.

"Christopher Hugh Roblanch," Chris said, folding his hands together atop the table. He shifted uncomfortably in the chair when Detective McDonough sat across from him and wrote down Chris's name.

You've got to do it for Alice, mate. Cool down, and tell them what's happened to her. You've got this.

"Okay, Christopher. What's your girlfriend's name?"

"Alice Julian."

McDonough wrote it down.

"You may know her as Alice Esposido, she called you earlier this afternoon," Chris said.

McDonough's pen stopped mid letter, his eyes widening. "Your girlfriend is the girl Alice, in the flat? We had some police go to her flat to arrest—"

"A burglar. Yes, she told me," Chris said.

"We sent police back to make sure she was all right. But when nobody answered, they knocked down the door, and she was gone. I assume you know what happened to her?" McDonough eyed Chris with a narrowed glare.

"Yes, sir." Chris wiped the sweat from his neck. He didn't know why he was nervous. He hadn't done anything wrong.

"What happened to her, Christopher?"

Without hesitation, Chris launched into the story. "Less than an hour ago, I learned Alice has been living in a dangerous situation her entire life. She told me her mother and step-father are addicted to drugs."

Detective McDonough wrote the details as they poured from his mouth. Encouraged by McDonough's nods, Chris continued.

"Alice's step-father has been bashing her up and molesting her since she was eleven-years-old." Chris stopped to let that sink in.

Detective McDonough's hand raced across the page taking notes on the notepaper. "Wait. What? How old is she? How old are you?"

"I'm eighteen, sir. She's seventeen," Chris said, holding McDonough's gaze.

His grey eyes widened, and his mouth fell open. "She's seventeen? This is despicable, we've got to do something." His voice rose with every word.

Chris rubbed at his stomach. *No kidding, it makes me ill. I wish I would bash her parents up.* "Detective, that's not the least of it. Alice has been sending me weird text messages the last few weeks. And tonight, she told me a man by the name of Andrew Carson has been trafficking her."

Detective McDonough stood, pulled his radio from his belt, and called other officers to join them. Within seconds, three police officers burst through the door behind Chris, making him jump. The officers crowded around Chris. Once Detective McDonough explained who Chris was and the situation, the other officers jumped into forming a plan of action.

"Where is Alice now?" Detective McDonough asked, tapping his pen on the pad of paper.

"She's at her best friend's house. She's been living there off and on throughout her life. She insisted on going there. Andrew told her if she left he'd kill her friend's mother, so she's trying to ensure she stays safe."

"What are these people's names?" McDonough asked, his pen at the ready.

"Krisany and Kahleesi Woodbury." Chris glanced down at his watch. "I'm terrified. She didn't want me coming here, because she thinks going to the police will only make matters worse, but I don't know what else I can do to protect her."

"Quick, you, Herbert, run over to the flat and see if Andrew and Layla Carson are there."

An officer pulled out his radio and ran out of the room.

"Andrew's wife, Layla, owns The Coral Clover." Chris swallowed the rising lump in his throat. "I don't know where their house is, but I'm terrified Alice or the Woodbury's are going to be hurt."

McDonough looked at the other officers. "All right, Snarr," he pointed at the officer. "Go to the Woodbury's, quickly. We can't take any chances after what Andrew Carson did seventeen years ago—he could do it again."

Chris jumped to his feet. "What did Andrew Carson do seventeen years ago?"

"I'm sorry," said McDonough, shaking his head, "but I can't share past investigations without permission." He caught officer Lockhart by the arm before he ran out. "Take your partner and stakeout the Carson's home, and send a team to check the Coral Clover as well."

The final officer left the room and shut the door. McDonough gestured for Chris to take his seat. "Thank you for telling us this, Christopher. It shows how much you care about Alice. Is there anything else we should know?"

"Not that I can think of." Chris clasped his hands together on the table and furrowed his brow. Had he missed anything?

"Christopher, we're going to do everything we can to help Alice, but you need to understand, it's normal for victims of trafficking not to trust. If she talks with a professional who has dealt with human trafficking and sexual abuse, she could get to a point where she will trust again, but it's going to take months—maybe years—for her to heal. Physical trauma often heals faster than emotional or psychological trauma. Those are much harder to overcome. The best advice I can give you is to start seeing a counselor as well. Perhaps, you ought to see someone together, if you think you are going to stay with Alice for a while. You need to learn how to help her—"

Someone rang Chris's mobile. Looking down, he narrowed his eyes.

"Is it Alice?" McDonough asked.

"Yes." Chris picked up the mobile and answered, putting it on speaker so McDonough could hear. "Hello."

"Chris, the police just rang the bell." Alice's tone dripped with a fury he'd never heard from her before, even after their many fights. "How dare you. I told you not to go talk to them. I bloody hate you."

"Alice, I—"

"Shut up, Christopher. You've put Krissy in even more danger. From now on, just stay the hell away from me, and my life." She sobbed.

Chris looked at McDonough. The man shook his head.

"Alice, darling, I didn't—"

"Shut up. You freaking lied to me."

He really hadn't lied. He just chose not to listen to her threat and do what his conscience told him was right.

"I don't want to see you again. Just stay away from me. Don't phone me. Don't text me, none of it. Do you understand?" Her voice shook.

"Alice, I only did it to protect you." Chris did his best to keep his voice calm. "I'm trying to be the good guy here," he whispered.

"Yeah right, Christopher. I have to go—the police want to question me. Thanks to you, idiot."

The call disconnected and Chris looked up, his eyes wide.

McDonough sighed and patted his shoulder. "She may come around, but you have to let her sort through all of this first. As far as she's concerned, you're on her enemy list with every other adult in her life, accept uh...Krisany," he said, scanning the pages of notepaper. "Give it time, and perhaps, things will work out for the best."

At the moment, he couldn't see how his relationship with Alice could ever be recovered, but he still felt coming here had been the right thing to do. Chris gave a slight nod and stood up, leaving Detective McDonough with his mobile number.

Chapter 21

Krisany walked into the lounge with her handbag swinging in her hands. "Alice, I want you to come with me to Wandsworth Prison again."

I clenched my hands into fists, heat rising into my cheeks. "Absolutely not! I am not going anywhere near my father. I never want to see that man again."

"Alice, I understand that you're upset with the way things happened the last time you met him, but I think you should give him another ch—"

"No." I had already given him another chance. I called him in my darkest hour, but he couldn't even bother to come to the phone. "And you can't make me. Go by yourself, since you're such good friends with him. I'm staying here."

Krisany raised her eyebrows, staring me down. "Alice, nobody hates Andrew Carson more than Jack Julian. He knows all about him, and he might have useful information that can help your case."

I sighed and gritted my teeth. "All right, fine. Let's go."

***

Krisany and I sat in familiar plastic chairs. I stared at the prison's dull gray walls, clenching my hands together. I tried to breathe deeply to calm my thudding heart, but it wasn't working.

"It's all right, Alice. Jack will listen to you once you tell him what happened." Krisany said.

I shook my head and blinked away tears, which threatened to spill over. Krisany put her arm around me and caressed my left shoulder. "You'll be fine, honey," she whispered. "I know you don't want to see your father right now, but he truly is a very sweet man."

I could only nod and stare at my clasped hands.

Our names were called, and I followed Krisany on shaking legs to the little, gray room where we had met Jack the first time.

Hatman looked at Krisany. "Do you want to stand?"

"Oh no, sir. I'll wait until Jack is here, and then I'll wait out there." She nodded toward the waiting area we had come from.

I sat at the sound of footsteps on the other side of the door. I didn't want to give Jack the impression I was overeager for this meeting, or that I respected him enough to wait for him to enter before finding a chair. His actions, or lack thereof, had killed any dreams I'd once had of a relationship with my father.

Jack stepped into the room. His handcuffs were removed and Hatman followed Krisany out without a word. Jack walked to the table and stood behind the last empty chair in the room. He placed his hands on its back, his hazel eyes drilling into my own.

"What are you doing here, Alice?" His rough voice sent a chill down my spine, but I was ready to fight.

"Jack, I've been in a living nightmare for long enough, so you're going to listen to me. I don't care about your prison rubbish, your stupid friends, or the decisions you made that ruined our lives. This is about me, not you."

"Whoa, hang on there." He stepped to the right, but stopped short of circling the table. "You don't get to come in here and talk to me with that attitude—"

"Shut the bloody hell up, Jack, and listen to what I have to tell you." I rose from my chair, clasping the edge of the table with both hands until my fingers hurt. My body shook, warmth rushing to my face. I looked into Jack's face, a mirror image reflected back at me. We stood in silence, holding each other with our piercing gazes.

"What on earth have you been through that's worse than what you've already told me? Wait. don't answer that. You don't know a fraction of my bloody story, so why should I listen—"

"Shut up, Jack and let me speak," I shouted.

"Stop shouting at me and tell me what happened." Jack circled the table, prowling like a caged animal toward me, but I refused to back down. "If you don't cool down, I will walk out of here, right now, and you will never hear from me again." Seeing him up close made my blood turn icy. My gaze slid to his fisted hands, and my throat tightened.

Nodding, I sat down in the chair and Jack returned to his. His eyes seemed to examine my every move. I glanced down at my clenched hands and focused on my breathing, getting my anger under control. "I should have listened to you."

"Listened to me about what?"

"Andrew Carson." I pressed my face into my hands and sobbed, unable to say more.

"Oh, my God." Jack jumped to his feet. "Alice, what happened?" He paced the floor, clenching his hands as he glared at the walls.

"We met at Beatrice's wedding. I think my mother called him Andrew, but I was so upset I had some ice lollies and ended up drunk. Then, Andrew referred to himself as Edward Dwight, and I had trouble sorting everything out."

Jack stopped mid-step to turn around and glared at me. "You what? Alice, are you mad? You're not even the legal age to drink. This is so bloody infuriating." The growling tone of his words scared me, but, to my relief, he went back to pacing.

"Andrew was so kind to me that night. He helped me get home, and the next day he returned to check up on me."

Jack sighed and rolled his eyes. "I told you before, that man is never to be trusted."

Yes, I should have been cautious, but, at the time, he looked like my only saving grace. After he overheard my step-father threaten to molest me again, Andrew offered me a flat."

Jack stopped pacing and stood as still as a statue, with his hands clenched. I didn't know what his stance meant so I kept explaining.

"I went with him because he was so charming. He was giving me what I needed, and said he'd keep me safe. I was desperate."

Jack nodded, the first positive reaction I'd seen from him so far.

"At first, Andrew and his wife did deliver on all their promises to take good care of me, until..." My voice broke with the new flood of tears pouring down my face.

Jack relaxed his hands and took tentative steps toward me. He stopped at my side, his eyes as blurry with welling tears as my own. "Alice, what happened?"

"He sold me for sex twice, before I escaped." I shook in the chair. Unsure of what to do, I remained where I sat, a complete wreck, but I didn't care. I couldn't look at Jack's face a moment longer, he scared the living hell out of me. I looked at my shaking legs instead.

"I thought I was protecting you by pushing you away, but now, it's clear, that was the wrong choice. Alice, stand up, sweetheart."

Sweetheart? The endearment seemed so odd coming from him, I found myself obeying. But if he tried anything, I'd bash him. "Alice, I'm sorry you ended up with Andrew Carson, and I'm sorry he trafficked you." Jack's shaking hand took hold of mine. His grip remained light so I didn't jerk away. "Your life has been a living hell because of me. I can't change what has happened to you. What you had to endure was horrific, but I promise, from now on, you have me." He bent, trying to get me to look him in the eyes. "I'm sure you've told everyone to get lost, right?"

I nodded, but refused to lift my head.

"I bet you want to tell me to get lost, too, yeah?"

"Uh huh." My body shook with another wave of tears.

"Come here." He pulled me into an embrace, and I was too exhausted to fight him. "I still can't believe you're my baby girl. This is incredible." His tone grew thick with emotion.

I slid my arms around his waist. "Jack?"

"Yes?"

"This is so messed up." Was I really going to just forgive this man who had rejected me so harshly the first time? Maybe if I was surrounded by more adults who wanted to really protect me, but I didn't have that luxury.

"Yeah, you're absolutely right."

"What are we going to do?" I sniffed.

"Alice, you've got to talk to someone about this—all of it. It's the only way you'll sort it out and be okay in the future. I wish I could have done that. Maybe I wouldn't have ended up here," he said with a grimace. "I know we don't have much of a relationship, and you have little reason to listen to me, but can you at least do this for me?"

I nodded and sniffed.

"Thank you, darling. I want you to be as successful as possible. The only way that will happen is if you sort this out." Jack sniffed and cleared his throat. "I also want you to remember one thing—I am so proud of you."

"Why? I've been used and treated like rubbish. I don't matter." I pressed my face into his shirt.

"Sweetheart, no. Don't say that." He patted my shoulder.

"But it's true." I cried. "Nobody cares about me."

"You know that's not true. I care about you."

"No you don't. You abandoned me, Jack." The truth of those words made me sob even harder.

He didn't say anything for a long moment, just held me close and cried with me.

"Alice, I wish I could do something more than say I'm sorry. I didn't know about you. Your mother lied about the results of the paternity test. Maybe if she hadn't, things could have been different for both of us, but I'm here for you now."

I lifted my head at his trembling tone. His eyes were filled with tears.

"You told me you didn't want to be a part of my life when we first met. Why the sudden change? How do I know you're not going to lie to me like everyone else?"

Jack's tears fell fast, mixing with my own on the dirty floor. "I said those things because I thought the best thing for you was to live your life without me. That's why I didn't take the call when you rang here. I'm sorry, angel. I'm not asking you to trust me, or even talk to me after this visit if you don't want to. But if you need me, I'll be here. I'll do all I can to support you, no matter what. All right?"

Nodding, I returned my face to his shirt and cried.

"Honey, it's going to be all right, but you have to tell the police everything, and I mean everything. It's the only way Andrew Carson will get the justice he deserves, and you'll finally be free of him."

"Okay." He was right. I needed to see Andrew Carson pay for what he'd done to me before I could truly begin to heal. I held onto Jack, crying until it was time to leave.

* * *

A few weeks later, my mobile rang.

"Hello."

"Hey, Alice. It's Jack, your father," said a rough voice on the other end of the line.

I laughed at the way he still referred to his new found fatherhood every time we spoke. "Oh hello, *father*. How are you?"

"Good. Listen, I contacted my Barrister, and she went to the prosecuting barrister in your case against Andrew Carson. She got me a deal to be released from prison for the time I have already served if I testify against Andrew. I just received the subpoena. I wanted to let you know that my Barrister, Shalise Rindi, and I will be there at the trial."

"That sounds wonderful." I couldn't think of anything better than having him there, in the flesh, to support me. And to be able to stay with me forever after the trial was over? Even better. "Thanks. Jack—uh...father." Maybe one of these days the word would stop sounding so foreign to me.

Jack chuckled. "You're welcome, sweetheart. I'll ring you again to see how you're doing in a couple days. I've got to go, it's bloody expensive to phone out of here. Love you, darling."

"Okay, love you, too." Smiling, I hung up my mobile and laid back on the pillows.

Well, you may be a convict Jack, but you're still my father. It will be nice to have you with me at the trial. I hope you and Andrew don't get into a fight. I hope Andrew doesn't come after me. Lord, that would terrify me. It's good to finally be safe.

CHAPTER 22

"Monster Knights" had to be Chris's favourite video game at the moment, especially when he was winning. Astride a flying horse, his character rained down terror wherever he went. An object entered the screen, a projectile launched from below. Chris hit a button to deflect the object with his shield, but lost his grip on the shield in the impact.

His mobile rang, distracting him from retrieving his shield before it disappeared in the dense forest below.

"Thanks a lot, person, I just lost one of my strongest defenses." He paused the game and picked up his mobile. Chris glowered at the name he saw, but he still couldn't bring himself to reject the call. "Alice, I thought you never wanted to speak to me again?"

"But I need you… I'm sorry, Chris. I blew it. I—n—need you." Her words trailed off to a whisper.

Chris shook his head. He was tired of being her go to whenever she found herself in trouble. It only ended up with him being yelled at. And he really couldn't handle that today. Yet, once again, he couldn't bring himself to hang up on her. "Is someone stocking you?"

"Thanks to you and your friends, the police, I'm perfectly safe."

"Good." He steeled himself against the sounds of her sniffing. He hoped, one day, her tears would have no effect on him. "Why are you ringing me?" He stood and looked out the large window where gray light poured in.

"I'm going to court—"

"Court? What happened?"

"With my dad—"

Chris dropped his mobile and it slid beneath the settee. Crumpling to his knees, he managed to get the mobile back after only a few swipes. He pressed it to his ear, gasping. "Why are you going to court with your dad? I thought you hated him." Who knew how much of the conversation he had missed, but he couldn't move on without understanding that development.

"He's testifying against Andrew...next Tuesday..." Her sobbing tears made it difficult for Chris to make out most of her words. "Please come... I'm...I'm scared...I need...need you... Can't face them alone..."

Her sobs grew so intense the rest of her explanation was a garbled mess. It didn't matter, he'd understood enough.

* * *

When Chris walked into the courtroom, Alice sat with a man and a barrister at a dark, wooden table. The guy had to be her father, no way would she sit that close to the man who had Trafficked her.

The man glanced at him when he approached. Chris chose to keep his eyes fixed on Alice, instead.

"Hello, Alice. How are you holding up?"

"Christopher, you came." Alice jumped up and leaned over the railing to hug him.

Jack also stood, a frown grooving his mouth. His dark eyes looked Chris up and down. "So you're Christopher?" he said, gruffly.

"Yes, sir." Chris extended his hand to the man the moment Alice stopped hugging him. "You must be Jack."

"Yes, I'm Alice's father." Jack stared at him, his gaze

unwavering. "Now listen, boy, you better not hurt her, or else you're not going to live to see the light of day. Understand? She's been through enough hell."

"I understand, sir." In fact, Chris wholeheartedly agreed with the man. "I promise, I'm not going to hurt Alice. I love her. She's a very special girl."

Jack glanced at Alice and a lopsided grin formed on his face. "Yeah, she is."

Chris took a seat on the tan upholstered chair, behind Alice. Krisany sat in the seat next to him. He offered her a quick nod, then focused all his energy on Alice. He willed his strength to her over the railing dividing them. She had expressed such nervousness on the phone this morning, he longed to physically hold her, but this would have to be enough.

A jingling sound caught Chris's attention. Jack had raised his shackled hands to rub her shoulder. At least her father was as in tune as a parent should be to the needs of his child. Her mother had totally failed her as a parent.

The dark, polished wood of the jury box held whispering people. Even the stenographer seemed to be nervous, click, click, clicking on the stenotype machine set up near the judge. The table across the aisle from Jack and Alice's barrister sat empty.

A chill ran down Chris's spine when the door at the back of the courtroom opened. Andrew Carson, his wife, Layla, flanked by their barrister and a police officer, were led past, to sit at the empty table.

Wearing a gray tracksuit, Andrew showed no remorse. He glared at Alice and those with her. His lips smirked when Jack's head turned toward him.

Alice swiveled in her chair, almost like she was preparing to run. Chris waved his hand, pleading with her to look at him. Her wide eyes fell on his face.

It's okay, he mouthed, gesturing for her to stay seated. *I'm right here. He can't hurt you anymore.*

Becoming aware of his daughter's distress, Jack opened his arms as wide as the handcuffs would allow and encircled them around Alice. He nodded at Chris, acknowledging his effort to help.

"All rise!" said a male bailiff who stood at the front of the room.

A door to the right opened, and a judge, wearing black robes, entered from his chamber. No one sat until he took his place on the bench.

"Julian against Carson," said the female stenographer, her fingers click, click, clicking as she spoke.

"Andrew Carson," said the judge, his loud voice carrying through the room with ease, "you are on trial for the trafficking of Alice Julian, who is here today. Mr. Carson, please rise."

Andrew stood up.

"I understand you are entering a plea in your case today?" The judge lifted his head, showing less of the top of his thinning, gray hair, to look through his spectacles at Andrew Carson.

"Yes, Your Honour." Andrew's voice held no emotion. Chris could not understand how that was possible with the charges he faced.

"Mr. Carson, let me remind you that your plea cannot be changed. Has your barrister reviewed this with you?"

"Yes, Your Honour."

"Very well. How do you plead?"

"Guilty."

Audible gasps and a buzz of conversation came from all around the courtroom. Alice and Jack exchanged open-mouthed gazes.

"Order." The judge banged his gavel. "Let it be shown on the record of Alice Julian Against Andrew Carson, Andrew Geoffrey Carson has pleaded guilty."

Click, click, click...from the court stenographer's stenotype machine was the only sound in the room.

"Before I leave to deliberate your sentence, Mr. Carson, do you have anything you would like to say?"

"Yes, Your Honour."

"All right. Please come to the stand where you may address us."

Andrew stood and made his way to the stand with a police escort. Once Andrew was sworn in, his green eyes darted from Alice to Jack, then around the courtroom. He held up a piece of notepaper and read. "It all started during my final term at Oxford." He looked up again to stare at Alice. "Alice, your dad had already received his degree and let me be his flatmate. We met Krissy and your good-for-nothing mother at a party being held by a mutual friend. Lord knows what on earth your father was thinking when he left the party to make love to Beatrice. At the time, I begged him not to do it, but he didn't listen." His voice rose and his gaze flickered to Alice once more. "You my dear, were the product of too much alcohol and their one night together. How do you feel about that? Neither of them wanted you, Alice."

Jack's handcuffs jingled again as he reached up to offer a comforting rub on her shoulder.

"Your dad wasn't himself after that," said Andrew, reading once more. "He thought money would be the answer to cure his loneliness. He hated girls, and wanted nothing to do with them after he saw what your mother was like, but that was to be expected. I wanted nothing more than to get your dad back to the fun-loving guy I liked to run with. He finally accepted one of my many invitations, and came with me to Hollow Joe's Pub. However, I was short for my portion of utility bills that month, and I knew your dad would throw me out if I came late with the money again. The plan I concocted roped your unknowing father into a situation, because he finally accepted my invitation for drinks." Andrew glanced at Jack and Alice. Sighing, he wiped perspiration from his brow.

"Alice, your father is innocent... I asked your dad to get us another drink, while I left to ask the cashier for some money. The girl refused to give me anything, so I killed her to get what I needed. I would have let your dad go, but he tried to help her. I didn't want to be caught, so I scuffled with your dad and made sure his DNA was also on the gun and left it behind.

I forced your father to drive me away. I started smoking weed but your dad took it away. It made me so angry, I devised a plan to kill us both. Besides, I didn't want him ratting me out. Unfortunately, we weren't the ones who died in the car crash. A couple by the name of Ian and Sylvia Frothington died when we slammed into them. Your dad almost bled to death from his injuries, and I wasn't about to be caught. I ran from the scene of the crime, leaving your father to take the fall for me. Your dad was wrongly accused of shooting the cashier because they couldn't tell whose finger or DNA was on the trigger of the gun. I was gone and your father was convicted—life for murder and vehicular manslaughter. He was a sweet man for taking the heat all these years. I went underground and built a new life, until I took you in. But you had to go to the police and tell them I trafficked you."

His growling tone made a chill run from Chris's head to his feet. He clenched his fists until his fingers hurt.

"I did traffic you, Alice. You were the best girl I've ever had. The men loved you. They couldn't stop talking about you. I had clients lined up for weeks out, but none of that matters. Once again, Jack Julian is innocent. I admit to everything and take full responsibility. I framed Jack Julian, and yes, trafficked his daughter, too. I did all of it!" Andrew shouted. "I've suffered the guilt, just like you Jack— for eighteen bloody years. Today, it's finally ending!" He threw the notepaper off the stand. It floated down to the tan coloured carpet.

"Is that all, Mr. Carson?" the judge asked.

"Yes, Your Honour," Andrew said, blinking away tears, his body shaking. He bit his bottom lip and his chest rose and fell.

"All right, you may be seated. Miss Julian, would you care to address us?" the judge asked, looking in Alice's direction.

"Yes, Your Honour." Alice looked at Jack. He gave her a broad smile.

A police officer escorted Andrew off the stand and back to his seat.

Alice made her way to the stand and stood front and center. She turned her head slowly to face Andrew and Layla Carson, her hazel eyes drilling into them before lifting a sheet of notepaper. Her fingers looked pale gripping its edges, but her voice sounded strong. "Today is a new beginning in my life. I met Andrew at my mother's wedding to my step-father. I was worried and scared about my future. At the time, his offer of a flat meant protection from those who wanted to harm me. I didn't realize it at the time, but he is just as lecherous. He and his wife groomed me with food, shelter, clothes, a modeling job—everything I needed to survive. I didn't even know I was being trafficked the first time it happened. I was told a clothing designer was coming to the flat. Helpless and alone, I suffered that man's advances. But, thank the Lord, I was able to escape the next day, and had my second client arrested. Being a prisoner to this couple has made me think about a lot of things. The importance of being able to truly be free and choose my life's direction. I'm going to finish college, and do all I can to be successful in life and put this nightmare behind me." Alice's eyes sparkled as she looked up from her paper.

"click click click click click click"

"Is that all you have to say, Miss Julian?" the judge asked.

"Yes, Your Honour," Alice said with a nod.

"Thank you. You may be seated."

"click click click"

A gasp in the courtroom caught Chris's attention. Looking to his right, Chris saw Andrew rise from his chair. Andrew's shackled hands grasped a pen from the table.

What the...Oh no.

Chris kicked over his chair and rushed to the center of the room, hoping he'd be able to get between Alice and Andrew Carson in time.

CHAPTER 23

I hadn't gotten very far from the stand when I froze. Andrew winked at me.

Why did he wink? His good looks and charm hide a sinister man far more terrifying than my father.

"Alice," Andrew said, "I may be going to prison, but I can still send someone after you. You're not safe, darling."

His cool voice sent a chill from my head to my feet.

Andrew unclenched his hands to reveal a black pen with a gleaming silver point. Holding the pen out in front of him, Andrew launched himself at me. The pen tore through the thin fabric of my light-green dress, a sharp sting piercing my shoulder. Andrew backed away, but the pen remained.

"Stay away from her." Chris barreled into Andrew's knees, knocking him to the ground. He pummeled his face, accentuating each punch with his words. "You're nothing but a thug, a bloody conman."

The growing stain of blood at my shoulder made me wobble. What a pathetic end to my life. I finally found the courage to stop allowing the adults in my life to hurt me only to die now.

Chris looked up and gasped. "Alice, you're bleeding!" He rushed to my side. "Come, let me look at your shoulder." He inhaled at the wound. "I need to get you out of here."

Scooped off my feet, I laid my head on Chris's shoulder and watched police officers constrain Jack from being able to pick up where Chris had stopped in his efforts to beat Andrew senseless.

"Wait," I said to Chris before he tried to barrel through the crowd with me in his arms. I couldn't leave until I was sure my father wouldn't do anything that might put his newly gained freedom in jeopardy.

"Jack," I called out with as much strength as I could muster in my weakened state, "you have to stop."

Jack stopped fighting the hands restraining him and looked at me with tears in his eyes. "I'm sorry, sweetie. You've been hurt again because of me."

"An ambulance is on the way," said one of the officers holding on to my father. "She's going to be all right."

How could the officer be so sure? My head was growing woozier by the second. If I lost consciousness, would I ever wake up again?

Another police officer bent to help Andrew to his feet. "Mr. Carson, get up!"

The moment Andrew stood, he threw his shoulder into the officer. The officer dodged the attack and Andrew head-planted into the stand. Andrew shook his head clear and tried again, this time bowling the officer to the floor.

Amidst the erupting screams, Chris carried me away to a distant chair. I watched in horror as Andrew wrestled the baton out of the police officer's holster. His quick swing connected with the downed officer, knocking him out cold. Would he be coming for me next?

Chris tried to gather me closer on his knee, but his actions brushed the pen still jutting out of my shoulder.

I groaned. "Please don't touch it, Chris."

"I'm sorry, I didn't mean... I'm sure an ambulance is coming, just hang in there, sweetie."

"This bloody hurts." The wet crimson on my aching arm had now reached my elbow.

I raised my tear stained cheek off Chris's shoulder. Andrew

had jumped over to the judge's bench and slammed the baton into the man's face, smashing the man's spectacles into his eyes. Blood gushed from the judge's nose.

An officer ran past, yelling into his radio. "We need an armed guard in courtroom three, now!"

I gasped, watching Andrew send the judge toppling over the bench, headfirst onto the floor below. Jack and Andrew's barristers rushed forward to help the judge until Andrew leaped onto the bench, raising the baton high in the air.

Clutching her hands together, Layla Carson ran toward her husband. "Honey, no, please don't! We'll make it through this together. Please Andrew, don't do this. Let us help you, love!"

Jack's voice thundered in front of me. "Andrew, you're an idiot! You're going to kill yourself and the rest of us in this courtroom if you don't cool down." His voice drowned out Layla's sobs and bounced off the courtroom walls.

"I've made up my mind. This is the only way! I confess to everything, to the car accident, the murder of the cashier in the pub." He looked toward Layla. "The trafficking that we did over the years, the embezzlement from the Coral Clover, and now." He choked back a sob. "Goodbye." He launched himself at the police officers below him, the baton poised to strike.

A door behind the judges bench burst open. A single gunshot brought silence to the courtroom.

Hatman grabbed Layla's right hand and pulled it behind her back. He looped handcuffs around her wrist and then grabbed her other hand and finished tightening the cuffs. "Well, that's a dying declaration if I've ever heard one. Layla Carson, you are under arrest for human trafficking and embezzlement. You have the right to remain silent…"

CHAPTER 24

Alice clung to Chris, almost choking him, but he did nothing to stop her. He didn't like looking at the blood pooling around Andrew's motionless body either. Looking away, Chris caught Jack staring at him. Maybe a wiser man would have extricated himself from the arms of his only daughter, but Chris drew Alice closer. He loved her, and nothing Jack did to intimidate him would change that.

The door at the back of the courtroom burst open and police and medical personnel stormed the room. Layla was escorted out of the room by two police officers, her shrieks fading away with her departure. Andrew Carson was also loaded onto a stretcher and taken away.

A woman, wearing a medical personnel uniform, bent down in front of Alice. "Can you turn more for me?" She touched Alice's back, nudging her to open up more. "Hmm…" Her prodding fingers around the protruding pen made Alice gasp in pain. "It's going to be okay." The woman looked up at Chris. "I'll take her from here."

"No. I don't want to go alone." Alice tightened her hold on Chris's neck.

"He is not authorized to ride in the ambulance," the woman said in a gentle tone.

Chris cupped Alice's face before she could argue more. "I promise. I will be at the hospital."

Chris glanced at the cooling pool of crimson drying on his shirt. The copper metallic smell knotted his stomach. He rose to leave, but the judge waved away medical personnel and began to speak.

"In lieu of the interesting testimony just received by the defendant, Mr. Carson. I am expunging Jack Julian's record—effective today." The judge looked at Jack. "As a newly free man, I hope you will be able to find a positive direction in your life. Court is—" The door at the back of the courtroom banged open and a police officer ran into the room. He gave a piece of notepaper to the judge.

The judge looked the notepaper over. "I've just been informed that Andrew Carson has been pronounced dead."

A buzz of conversation hummed around the room, but Chris wasn't happy the man had gotten out of going to jail for his crimes.

The judge walked over to his desk and banged the gavel. "Order. On behalf of the courts, our thoughts go out to the defendant's family for the sudden loss of the defendant. We'll take a better look at security to ensure this type of incident never happens again. Thank you to the prosecuting and defending barristers for your time. This case is adjourned."

Chris needed to get to the hospital for Alice, but seeing the awe in Jack's face as the officers removed his handcuffs stopped him. As a free man, maybe he would like to join him.

***

Chris shared the news about Andrew's death to help Alice find peace, yet it seemed to have the opposite effect. She sat up straighter, lifting away from the hospital pillows propping her up.

"I don't understand why this had to happen. Andrew was a coward. He took the easy way out, rather than suffer like you had to." She pointed at her father who stood on the other side of the bed with his head bowed. "It's not fair! I want to curse him out for everything he's done to us. I hate him, and I hate you for getting us into this mess."

"Alice," Chris said, gently pushing her back onto the pillows but making sure to avoid the bandaged wound. "If you don't calm down, they'll make us leave." Maybe he shouldn't have brought her father along afterall.

"I'm sorry, Alice, truly I am. If I had known you existed, none of this would have happened. Darling, I promise, I'll be there for you the best I can," Jack said, wiping a tear away with his fingers.

"Jack, I'm not sure how close I want to be with you." She reached for Chris's hand.

He gave her a supporting squeeze, but refused to say anything. Coming from a messed up family of his own, Chris understood how personal this decision was. He didn't want to influence her one way or the other.

"I understand," Jack said. "You have the right to decide if you want me in your life or not. I don't ever want you to feel like I'm intruding. But please know that I'm here for you and I'll support you in whatever you decide." He stepped closer. "Most of all, I want you to know that I'm proud of you. Alice, you've overcome so much. You've had to live in hell your entire life, and yet you're flourishing. You're a beautiful young lady, and I can't wait to see where you go in your life."

"Thanks, Dad." Alice let go of Chris's hand and reached for her father. He responded quickly, bending down to hug her close. She sobbed into his shirt.

"I love you, honey. Do you have a middle name?"

"Yeah, Brianna," she said, lifting her head.

"Oh, that's beautiful…Alice Brianna." Jack pulled back and smiled. "Where did Brianna come from?"

"Beatrice liked the name. She said it rolled off the tongue quite well."

Jack chuckled. "Well, I think it's beautiful."

Chris thought it was beautiful too, but he kept the comment to himself. There would be plenty of time in their future together for him to tell her later.

Chapter 25

My father's new found freedom, really a sad, rundown flat, wasn't much to look at. I sat on his latest procurement, a second-hand settee, wringing my hands.

Even after two months, I still struggled to put the whole horrid ordeal behind me. Just like the wound on my shoulder, though healed, a scar still remained.

I should have listened to my dad's warning to stay away from Andrew, but I pushed his warning aside like a cold cup of tea. Rather than help me, Andrew had thrown me into a new nightmare, yet, somehow, I managed to survive and free myself.

I was nearly done with Edgington College, and the summer-term swim gala would take place next weekend. I was looking forward to it. A solid performance would help me reach my goals of swimming at the university level. My hair and skin smelled of chlorine. I needed a shower, but the time had come to face my father. He'd given me more than enough time to consider the direction I wanted our relationship to go.

Over the last two-months, I had been trying to decide if I wanted my dad in my life or wanted to write him off like Chris had done with his biological mum, Aaliyah. Part of me wanted Jack in my life, but every time I tried to build up the courage to tell him I would panic and think of reasons to say no, to keep him away.

My dad had told me he would accept whatever I told him, but I didn't believe him. This would be our fourth time being in the same room together, though we had spoken on the phone a few times. If only there was a way I could be sure he wouldn't let me down one day. The pain of betrayal that I had experienced throughout my life, like lava, had scorched every inch of it, and more than once.

I don't think I want you in my life right now, dad. There's too many unknowns. I need to graduate college and prepare for university, and I don't think I can do that with you in my life at present.

I shivered beneath the black T-shirt and shorts I wore, the air conditioning blowing directly on me.

Please understand what I tell you, father.

My father returned from his little kitchen, carrying a tray and two mismatched cups. "So, how are your studies going?" As always, his voice was rough and low.

"Good." I took a cup from the tray he lowered toward me. "I won my swim competition this morning. It puts the girls in line to have a solid chance for placing in the summer-term swim gala next week."

Jack sat on the settee, but not so close to make me uncomfortable. "I'm glad you've had swimming to distract you. I've been thinking about the trial for the last two months. I can't get Andrew off my mind." He leaned back and glared at the ceiling.

"Yeah, swimming is a good distraction, but I've thought about Andrew, too. Even now, I still think he was a bloody coward."

Jack chuckled. "Yes, he was. You are an incredible girl, Alice… You were able to escape him." His gaze turned to me, but, rather than look away, I nodded and smiled.

The silence stretched on, growing uncomfortable with nothing but the clock ticking on the wall behind me.

"Has Beatrice said anything to you?" Jack said.

My mother wasn't a subject I loved to discuss, but it was better than silence so I readily answered. "Yes, she's constantly texting me to see if I'm going to press charges against Miguel. I've told her no, even though I intend to do the opposite. Beatrice can't run my life anymore, and it's time Miguel paid for the hell he put me through for the last seven years. Watching him be charged and go to prison is the only way I'm going to find closure with that filthy little man. He's a sex maniac and I was his slave, but no more. Beatrice was too much of a narcissist, and a bitch to ever really love me."

Jack grinned. "Amen! You're brilliant, you are. I'm so proud of you. I can't even imagine what you've gone through. It's absolutely horrifying."

"Yeah, it was horrible, but it's better now. I took your advice and I'm going to counseling, and that's helping, just like you said it would. Chris, Krissy, and her daughters have been really helpful, too," I said, twirling strands of my curly wet hair around my fingers.

"I'm glad to hear you're talking about the life you've been living with a professional—that's the best thing you can do for yourself." Jack rubbed his temples and glanced up at the clock. "How are things with Chris? I'd really like to have a chat with him and see what he's like."

"He's fine, we're thick as thieves. If you want to have a chat with him you can, he's outside. He came to my swim competition." I smiled, trying to ease into the next point I wanted to make. "But first, I need to talk to you about something, dad."

"Of course, what is it?"

"It's about us and our relationship." I stared into his ever-present gaze and sighed. "Dad, I'm not sure how to tell you this, but right now, I'm not ready to have you in my life. I need to prepare for the swim gala next week, graduate college, and prepare for university. Plus, after everything I've been through, I'm not sure if I should trust you. I hope you understand."

He stood up and helped draw me to my feet. His touch was so gentle I didn't fight him. "Alice, I completely understand why you're not ready for me to be in your life. Just know that I'll be here for you if that ever changes. There's no conditions on my end. You can choose how close you want us to be. I know you have a lot going on and you need to take some time to sort out everything that you've been through in the last seven years. That's going to take time, but as your father, my love for you will never change. Even if you decide not to have anything to do with me ever again, it's entirely your choice, darling. All right?"

"Okay, thanks, dad. I hope we can have a relationship in the future, but we'll have to see what happens. You seem like a nice person, but for now, my answer is no."

"I understand, love," Jack said with a smile.

The tension inside me melted away like ice cream on a hot summer's day. "Oh, what a relief. I love you, dad." I blinked at tears beginning to pool in my eyes.

"I love you, too, Alice." He patted me on the back.

"Would you like to meet Chris, now?" I asked when our arms dropped.

"Of course!"

"All right." I sat on the settee and sent Chris a text message.

CHAPTER 26

Jack held back the door to his small, crappy flat. Yeah, the place wasn't much to look at, but after years of being incarcerated, he considered it Buckingham Palace. He sized Chris up as he entered. Alice may not want him in her life right now, but he still wanted to protect her. He would just have to be covert in his efforts. "Christopher, nice to see you again. How are you?"

"Hello, sir, it's nice to see you again. I'm doing great. Nearly done with college, thank the Lord." Chris smiled at Alice, who had risen from the settee to greet him. "I think we need a break, eh, cutie pie?"

Cutie pie? This boy had guts to address his daughter in such a way with him present. Of course, he probably didn't see him as a father any more than Alice did at the moment.

Alice returned his smile with one of her own. "Yes, definitely."

"It's amazing we've made it to this point, after all the drama we've gone through this year." Chris added with a laugh.

Alice joined him in the chuckle, but Jack wasn't so sure being bound by common drama was such a good thing. Alice deserved and needed a stable boy, not more drama in her life.

"Chris, I would love to know more about you," Jack pointed to the settee, infusing his tone with enthusiasm. Hopefully, Chris wouldn't catch on that this was an interrogation. "What can you tell me about your family?"

Alice sat in her original spot on the settee. Chris sat next to her in the middle, which left a side of him open for Jack to crowd into his personal space without it looking intentional. What luck.

"I have a big family," Chris said. His brows furrowed when Jack also sat on the small settee.

True, he could have dragged one of the beat up chairs over from the tiny kitchen table, giving them more space, but this was so much more fun.

"My—my dad," Chris stuttered before gaining enough confidence to continue, "had to start over with me and my little sister Kanene after Aaliyah, our biological mother, ran out on us. About a year later, my dad married Tara, our mum. She brought three kids to the family, Emmalyn, Kenneth, and Gavin. Then, Tara and my father had a baby together, Erin."

"Oh wow, that's a big family you've got there." Jack liked the idea of Alice associating with someone who had such a large support system. He was sure it would still mean chaotic moments, but at least she wouldn't be alone.

"Yeah, it's loud, but it's fun." Chris laughed. "I work at a bakery and have been saving up money for university."

"Terrific." The boy didn't just have plans, but had put into action ways to attain those goals. Jack hoped he wanted to do something worthwhile with his life. "What do you want to study at university?"

"Chris wants to be an architect," Alice chimed in, squeezing Chris's hand.

An Architect? It was a much harder profession to make a living in than engineering, and usually fraught with people who only thought about the aesthetics of life rather than the foundations it took to make a life solid and lasting. "I see... Chris, I don't want you distracting Alice during your studies." He would probably have lots of free time. Jack couldn't imagine it took much to become an architect. "I want her to get an education, it's really important to me."

"Don't worry, sir, we both want to get our education."

Jack nodded. At least Chris wasn't planning on denying Alice her own opportunities for an education, though, only time would tell if she ended up supporting him.

"Did you go to university?" Chris asked.

"Yes, I went to Oxford, graduating with a degree in engineering." At one time, Jack thought that fact alone showed his superior intelligence, but not anymore. "The rest you heard at Andrew's trial." He sighed and glared at the ceiling. "If I could do it all over again, things would be different." Alice never would have had to grow up without knowing her father, and she would trust him now.

"That's brilliant that you have your degree," Chris said with a smile.

Jack laughed. "Yes, but it's of little use to me now."

Nobody laughed along with him. Jack cleared his throat, the silence growing unbearably awkward. The only thing he could think to get out of the situation was to change the subject. "Alice, I think you ought to consider becoming an advocate for human trafficking." Alice pressed her lips into a thin line, but he forged ahead. The idea had been swirling around inside him for weeks now. "Just think about it for a moment. If someone asked you about your story, what would you say?"

"I don't know. I have a lot of thoughts, but I need to organize them. I can say this, though—Andrew Carson didn't win, I did." The return of Alice's smile made Jack happy, watching Chris stroke her hand made him a little less so.

Jack sighed and lifted his eyes to his daughter's face. "That's right, Alice. You're going to do great things."

"Thanks dad." Alice said, her cheeks colouring red.

"And I agree." Chris threw his arms around Alice's shoulders and kissed her.

Chris's hand rubbing hers was something he could ignore,

but watching him accost her lips was too much, even for an uninvolved father like him. Jack cleared his throat. At least the boy had enough wisdom to pull away at the slight sound.

"Chris, what are your intentions with Alice?" Jack leaned in slightly more. This was a serious concern of his and he wanted him to know it.

"My intentions with your daughter are to love her, and be her friend. I never want to hurt her, especially after all the hell she has been through in her life. It's horrifying."

Jack grimaced at the words, but nodded. "Indeed, Alice has pulled through quite remarkably." He ran his fingers through his hair. "You promise you really care for her, boy?"

"Yes, I do."

"I love him, dad." Alice grabbed his hand in such a possessive way, Jack knew separating them wasn't going to be a possibility. "He's been there for me, through all of this. I was sure he'd run when he heard I was being trafficked, but he stayed."

True, he did stay. And that kind of commitment spoke volumes to Jack.

"I couldn't leave you, cutie pie." Chris grabbed her chin and gave it a loving tweak.

Cutie Pie? Jack wasn't sure how he felt about the endearment. Did Chris see Alice as someone he could manipulate, throwing out cute nicknames to desensitize her ability to think critically about their relationship? Sadly, he hadn't spent enough time with his daughter to even know if he should be worried. He sighed. "Chris, I'm going to be frank with you, I'm struggling to trust you. But, to be honest, I barely know Alice, either." Jack smiled at Alice. "I'm hoping that this is something that will change as the years go by." Jack turned his gaze back to Chris. "It'll be in your best interest not to hurt Alice, or we're going to have a huge problem. Understood?"

"I understand, sir," Chris said, slinging an arm around Alice's shoulders. Again, Jack wasn't thrilled with the touchy feely, but Alice leaned closer to him.

"That's good. But I'd like to keep in touch with you to make sure you're keeping to your word." Jack really didn't have the right to demand such a request since Alice wasn't letting him officially into her life, but he couldn't stop himself from asking.

"That's fine," Chris said with a smile.

His quick agreement only helped him like the boy more. At least he had another way of keeping tabs on his daughter.

**

Walking to the car park, Chris glanced down at Alice. "That went well."

"Yeah, it did. He really cares about me," she said with a smile.

"Yes, he does, and so do I." Chris leaned down for another kiss, but Alice put a hand on his chest.

"You tell me that every day."

"What's wrong?"

"Nothing, I want to thank you for the millionth time, because I couldn't do any of this without you."

"Alice, you're so sweet." Chris kissed her forehead. "For growing up in such chaos, it's quite remarkable, honestly."

"Right back at you, Christopher." They shared a laugh, her hand wrapping around his waist.

Bending down, Chris kissed her on the lips, the smell of chlorine drifting to his nose. None of it was a turnoff, not with the bright sun draping its heat over them.

You're finally mine, Alice. All mine...

EPILOGUE

I sat on the tan fabric settee in the flat I shared with Chris. A football match played on the television. Chris kept glancing up from his maths textbook to yell at his team. It wasn't going to be a good night if they kept losing.

The heat from my laptop warmed my bare legs, drawing my gaze back down. I read over the statement I would read in court the following week. After everything that happened during my last court appearance, I wasn't eager for a repeat, but I refused to let my step-father, Miguel have his day in court without me. The judge would hear my personal account of all he had done to me over the years.

My mother hadn't spoken to me since Miguel had been arrested, but I didn't care. That relationship had sailed years ago.

Glancing at Chris, I noticed he was staring at the television again. That homework wasn't going to do itself, so I gave him a subtle reminder. "How is the maths coming?"

"I finished it. How does your statement look? Sorry about the yelling, but they don't know what they're doing. It's infuriating. Kick the ball you—"

My laughter stopped him before he swore. "Babe, you're cute when you're angry."

"Thanks, baby. I'm glad you're amused. Do you want me to look at that?" He pointed to my laptop screen.

"Yeah, thanks, but I'm not offering to check your maths. You're more advanced than me."

He gave a lopsided smile and took the laptop from my knees. I picked up a biscuit from the plate on the table next to me and took a bite.

A few minutes later, Chris handed the laptop back to me. "It looks good. I just made a few changes. I'm really proud of you. You're going to make Miguel pay for the crimes he committed against you, not to mention the drug charges he's going to face." He picked up his teacup and took a drink. "Could you hand me one of those biscuits?"

I kept scrolling through the document, looking over his editing corrections, but still managed to toss him a biscuit at the same time.

"Thanks," he said.

Chris's intelligence was on full display on my laptop. Him coming into my life was one of the best things that had ever happened to me. "You know there's no way I would have survived college without you, Krissy and her family, and the rest of our friends. I didn't want any of you around, but—" I glared at Chris, "—you forced me to let you in."

He laughed. "Babe, I wasn't about to let you go. You're stuck with me. What do you think about that?" He shoved the rest of the biscuit into his mouth.

"I'm thrilled," I said, though the admonition still made heat rise into my cheeks. "What a year for both of us. You dealing with Aaliyah and her drama, me escaping Beatrice and Miguel, having to escape a worse situation in Andrew and Layla, the mess at Andrew's trial, winning the summer swim gala for Edgington, moving in together and preparing to start university, and a second trial coming up for Miguel. Thank the Lord we're in counseling."

"No kidding, our lives are like a bloody soap opera, someone should write a book about us." Chris laughed. "Are you nervous to testify against Miguel?" He took my hand, his warm fingers broadening the smile on my flushed face.

"No, I'm not worried." I would have him with me, and that made all the difference in the world. "His threats are a distant memory now. Honestly, I think Andrew and Layla were my biggest challenge to overcome, but I had to get away from Miguel and Beatrice to realize it. Incest and human trafficking are horrible, but being worked to death is something I would have never survived. The nice thing is, I don't have to worry about any of that, anymore. I have wonderful friends, and a wonderful guy to help me out," I said, holding his gaze.

"Awe, thanks, baby."

I'm so glad I'm starting my life over with him. Growing up, my mother and step-father were addicted to drugs. I was molested, physically and verbally abused by my step-father during my teenage years. What Layla and Andrew did to me only added to my suffering, but being a prisoner to this couple, made me realize a lot of things. We need to be mindful of trafficking in our communities so we can help protect the innocent victims who are being trafficked all around us. Trafficking occurs in all communities, it happens to people from all walks of life, men, women, and children…nobody is immune to it. It was our responsibility to watch for the signs and let the police know if we saw anything suspicious or suspect something was going on. Only by working together would trafficking ever be stopped. And it was a message I would never stop sharing until the evil of trafficking was eradicated from society for good.

Resources

If you or someone you know is struggling with human trafficking, the following resources are available to help.

<u>England</u>

https://www.citizensadvice.org.uk/immigration/trafficking/report-human-trafficking/

If there's an emergency call 999, or 101 if it's not urgent.

If you suspect a child is in danger of being trafficked call the NSPCC 24 hour helpline 0808 8005 000

Report modern slavery to The Salvation Army 24 hour Confidential Helpline 0300 3038 151

The Modern Day Slavery Foundation's helpline is open 24 hours a day 0800 0121 700

***

<u>The United States of America</u>

https://www2.ed.gov/about/offices/list/oese/oshs/factsheet.html

If it's an emergency call 911, or your local police department if it's not urgent.

Report crimes at 1-866-347-2423 or submit a tip online at <u>www. ice.gov/tips</u>

National Human Trafficking Hotline - <u>https://humantrafficking hotline.org/node</u>

    Call: 888-373-7888
    Text 'help' to 233733

To report sexually exploited or abused minors, call the <u>National Center for Missing and Exploited Children</u>'s (NCMEC) hotline at 1-800-THE-LOST, or report incidents at <u>http://www. cybertipline.org</u>

To learn more about Jack, keep a lookout for Book 3 in The Hidden Hearts Series. Go to www.facebook.com/AuthorMacyLewis for updates.

***

The author has researched British vocabulary terms and phrases, the British legal system, and consulted with experts about sexual abuse and human trafficking. All people, circumstances, events, and places are from the author's imagination.

9 781480 894303